The V

Max Hennessy was the pen-name of John Harris.
He had a wide variety of jobs from sailor to
cartoonist and became a highly inventive, versatile
writer. In addition to crime fiction, Hennessy was
a master of the war novel and drew heavily on his
experiences in both the navy and air force, serving
in the Second World War. His novels reflect the
reality of war mixed with a heavy dose of conflict
and adventure.

Also by Max Hennessy

The Martin Falconer Thrillers

The Fledglings
The Professionals
The Victors
The Interceptors
The Revolutionaries

The RAF Trilogy

The Bright Blue Sky
The Challenging Heights
Once More the Hawks

The Captain Kelly Maguire Trilogy

The Lion at Sea
The Dangerous Years
Back to Battle

The Flying Ace Thrillers

The Mustering of the Hawks
The Mercenaries
The Courtney Entry

The
VICTORS

JOHN HARRIS WRITING AS
MAX HENNESSY

CANELO

First published in the United Kingdom in 1975 by Hutchinson Junior Books

This edition published in the United Kingdom in 2022 by

Canelo
Unit 9, 5th Floor
Cargo Works, 1-2 Hatfields
London, SE1 9PG
United Kingdom

A CIP catalogue record for this book is available from the British Library.

Print ISBN 978 1 80032 845 7
Ebook ISBN 978 1 80032 080 2

Look for more great books at www.canelo.co

Printed and bound in Great Britain by Clays Ltd, Elcograf S.p.A.

Chapter 1

I'd always thought of the King as a taller man, more imposing, more regal. Perhaps the impression came from the portraits I'd seen of him, those elongated flattering paintings which always made royalty look heroic. In fact, he was quite small and slight, but his eyes, those rather protuberant eyes Edward VII had also had, were shrewd and missed nothing.

'We are grateful, Mr Falconer,' he'd said.

The wound stripe on my sleeve wasn't very big but he hadn't missed it and he seemed to be watching me with fatherly concern.

'And what do you propose to do now?' he went on.

The words wouldn't come at first. I was terrified. I was still only nineteen and though I'd shot at, and been shot by, the King's enemies, it took all my courage to face the King himself, and I'd been

1

in a sweat ever since they'd told me to attend the investiture.

Behind the King was Green Park and the trees, and a faint breeze ruffled the curtains and carried with it the noise of the traffic outside. I still couldn't get the words to come but the King made no attempt to hurry me. I expect he'd had plenty of other young men in front of him, speechless with awe and the fear of doing something wrong, between August, 1914, and that February day in 1918.

The words came at last. 'I expect I shall be going back to France, sir,' I said.

'Don't you think you've done enough for a while?' he asked. 'I'm told that wound of yours was painful.' He paused then looked up at me again with a smile. 'I also understand it's not the policy to allow escaped prisoners of war back to the front in case they're captured again and made to suffer. Will they let you go?'

I wasn't sure they would. After a tour over the trenches in 1916 on every kind of ancient box kite you could think of, and another in 1917 in Pups, that had ended abruptly with a forced landing behind the German lines, and my being taken prisoner and wounded as I'd scrambled back to freedom, they'd decided I'd had enough for the time being and could stay where I was in England.

All through hospital I'd been trying to reverse the decision. Ludo Sykes, who'd escaped with me and had a little influence here and there, had pulled a few strings and, if nothing else, at least now there were a few people listening with sympathetic ears. It wasn't much but it was something to go on with, and was enough to enable me finally to make my reply with optimism.

'I hope so, sir,' I said.

At that moment there was nothing more I wanted in the world than to offer my life for that small, bearded, none-too-regal figure. Perhaps we were all too emotional, and patriotism during the war had been somewhat over-developed by the popular press, so that George V had become the symbol of the whole struggling war-weary country. But I was still barely out of the stage when I'd read Henty with enthusiasm, and derring-do and faithfulness to a cause were all important. I'd grown up a lot since I'd chased off to war in 1915 in a panic that it would be over before I got there, and I'd seen too much for the attitude to stick;

my brother had been killed with many other men I'd admired, and by 1918 there wasn't much left beyond cynicism and the wry self-deprecation at being caught that was the mark of all old soldiers. It said a lot for the King that he had the ability to reach beyond it to emotions I'd almost forgotten existed.

Afterwards, when it was all over and I was drawing relieved breaths outside, Charley appeared. Because my parents were involved with war work and hadn't been able to come down from Norfolk, I'd invited Charley, who was nursing at the First London General at Camberwell. There hadn't seemed to be anybody else, because Ludo Sykes, who in a way had filled my brother's place, had been sent to the north of Scotland to organize a new training school. With him he'd taken Jane Widdows, who was the only other person left in Fynling village that I knew. They'd been married while I was still in hospital and it had been Sykes' cousin, Charley – or to give her her full name, Charlotte Margaret Caroline Bartelott-Dyveton-Sykes, which was quite a mouthful and explained why she preferred plain Charley – who had stood nearby to hand me the crutches they'd insisted on me using, so I could be best man.

It seemed odd to think of Sykes, aloof, aristo-cratic, moneyed and confident, whom I'd admired since I'd first met him in 1915, married to Jane, whose hair I'd pulled and whom I'd taken fishing and taught to climb trees. But it had had the effect also when I went home of leaving me lost and empty and, like so many other young men on leave, with the unhappy feeling that home was no longer in England but in some obscure village in France. In four years, the place had changed. Jane's father, who farmed the land round Fynling, was tired and too busy with the shortage of labour to stop and talk, my parents never seemed to be home, and my brother had been dead for two years, while Jane's sister, Edith, whom he was once to have married, was married to a doctor now and in Northern Ireland. Even the pubs seemed to contain no one I knew, and the only thing the landlord seemed able to say was the usual 'What! You on leave again?'

Fortunately, if Fynling and my world had changed, so also, thank God, had Charley. When I'd first met her the previous year she'd been seventeen, gay, brittle, fashionable and full of all the up-to-date things to do and say, and I'd spent several week-ends with her in London, going down by train from where we'd been stationed with those awful BE12s as part of the defence of the capital against Zeppelins. We'd gone to tea-dances a lot but, as I always danced like a man with two wooden legs, it was lucky for me that she had a sense of humour, and the cinema was always much more of a success. She'd been a giggler in those days and it had been her big moment when I'd first kissed her – because she said she'd never been kissed by a pilot – but everyone had grown up fast in 1917, with the slaughter of Passchendaele leaving its mark on almost every family in the land, and she'd finally gone off to be a nurse. Like most VADs of her class, she'd expected her job would be to hold the patients' hands and smooth their pillows while the regular nurses, who came from a different strata of society, fetched and carried anything that looked or smelled unpleasant, and it was to her credit that when she found this wasn't the case she stayed where she was. It had changed her quite a lot, though, and although she could if necessary still say all the bright up-to-date things that were expected of a girl from her background, which was

Roedean and county shows, her work had sobered her and her giggles had turned instead to quiet and sometimes rueful laughter. Like Sykes himself, she could charm the ducks off the water when she tried, but this was a gift she kept only for flower-sellers who looked cold, London bobbies who were inclined to be awkward, and lonely elderly gentlemen who made passes at her. Mostly she was brisk, noisy and so full of all the latest ejaculations you'd have thought she hadn't a brain in her head.

Because she only had the day off, we were a bit limited about how we could celebrate the medal they'd given me. Charley was unperturbed, however. She was one of nature's optimists.

'It doesn't matter a bit, Martin,' she said. 'It's spiffing to see you and I might not have got the day off, and you might have been dead, not just wounded.'

Which was quite a point.

There was one other thing that bothered me, and had been bothering me ever since they'd first allowed me out of hospital. Would they let me fly again?

Since 1915, flying had become so much a part of my life, I just couldn't think what it would be like without the smell of petrol and burnt castor oil and dope and the sounds of the airfield I'd got to know so well – the tick of an engine as it cooled after being switched off, the tack-tack-tack of a machine gun being tested at the butts, and the distant bark of one of the dozens of dogs that always seemed to infest army camps. I couldn't imagine life without them.

Charley broke in on my thoughts. She looked surprisingly pretty in her uniform – blue-eyed, blonde, as English as a cottage garden, and suddenly bewilderingly mature. Despite the 'ups' and 'downs' we'd had we'd never quite lost touch from the day we'd first met – not even when I'd gone back to France – and we'd exchanged quite a few letters in our time.

'I suppose we ought to wet its head,' she said. 'After all, it isn't every day a girl gets the chance to be seen walkin' in London with a man with as many medals as you've managed to collect.'

'They always give you something for escaping,' I said. '"Ten for effort" sort of thing.' I grinned. 'And one of the others is a tidgy little thing the Belgians gave me because they happened to be visiting the aerodrome and they'd run out of people to give 'em to. I think they wanted to throw away the bag they were carrying 'em in.'

She stared at me, shocked. 'I don't believe it,' she said. 'And I think it calls for something.'

I hedged and she knew at once I had other things on my mind. 'You're shyin' like a young mare faced with a new rider,' she said. 'Any minute now you'll whinny and show the whites of your eyes.'

I laughed. 'There's something I have to do first.'

'Find out when you can go back to battle, murder and sudden death?' She said it with a smile but behind it there was the ancient wisdom of women that made me feel stupid and young and silly.

'How did you know?' I asked.

'I always know there's somethin' behind your fate-worse-than-death act and, knowin' you, it doesn't take much to guess what it is. Sometimes, Martin Falconer, I think you're probably not right in the head. You needn't, you know. Not now.'

'I know I needn't. But I couldn't live with myself if I didn't try. Besides—' I managed a sheepish grin '—I want to go on flying.'

'It's amazin' how you go all starry-eyed about that,' she said. 'I think if you and Ludo were up in the air when the last trump sounded, you'd need a nudge to come down and face the music.'

'What rot!'

'It isn't rot. Here I am eager to celebrate somethin' excitin' and brave and all you can produce is an attitude that's uncooperative in the extreme. It's enough to give a girl the pip.' She shrugged and gave me an engaging grin. 'What do I do? Sit in some draughty corridor at the fount of authority and wait?'

'That's it exactly.'

As good as her word, she took her seat on a bench by the porter's desk and settled down with a cigarette. The cigarette made the porter blink a bit but all the girls had taken to smoking since the war so he had to accept it.

The man I went to see I'd met once or twice briefly during my career. He was a great deal senior to me but he was distantly connected with Ludo's family and Charley's family and he was very sympathetic. I laid my question smack on the desk in front of him.

'Will they let me go back?'

He smiled, lit a cigarette and rubbed his nose while he considered. 'It could be arranged,' he said slowly, 'though no one captured in France has so far ever been allowed to fly there again.' He gestured. 'If they captured you again, you see, they might just consider you were an enemy agent and, in any case, there's always the serious probability of your being harshly treated.'

'Perhaps they'll *not* capture me.'

'Nice thought, of course,' he agreed. 'But since the prevailing wind over the lines blows from our side to theirs, capture's one of the things that's most likely to happen to a pilot.'

Since he wore wings, I had to admit he probably knew what he was talking about.

'However,' he went on, 'there *are* ways round all that. For instance, a paybook carried by you specially for flying could be made out in some fictitious name.'

'Would they allow that?'

'They might. After all, you've committed enough mayhem over the trenches for them to consider you might still be of some value to England. If only to show other people how to go about things.'

Like all the Sykeses, he was very languid but, also like the Sykeses, he was no fool. 'What do I do, then?' I asked.

'You don't,' he smiled. 'You're due to be posted to a training squadron in Yorkshire.'

'Training squadron!' I exploded. 'What for?'

'Because you were a prisoner of war and all prisoners of war are considered to be out of touch on return.'

'They only had me for two or three days.'

'You were behind their lines longer than that.'

'Two or three weeks.'

'Things change fast.'

'Not that fast,' I said. 'I don't need training. I've been flying for three years, most of the time in action.'

He grinned. 'Actually, it's a mere formality and you'll find yourself instructing within twenty-four hours. But the general trend is not to allow anyone to go back who's been captured. So obviously the sensible thing to do is to be like Brer Rabbit, and lay low and say nothin'. Eventually, they'll forget you and then you'll probably find yourself smuggled through in a batch of pilots being sent out to squadrons. I promise you I'll personally attend to it. But it'll need time.'

And that's how it had to stand.

Charley was sympathetic. 'You look as if you've been orphaned,' she said. 'Never mind, though, I'll get a posting up to Yorkshire, too, so you'll have someone's hand to hold when you come off duty in a bad temper.'

—

Settling down to instructing was easier said than done. Teaching raw pilots how to stay in formation after flying in France was like riding a bus into the city every day. It was repetitious and dull and we'd long since skimmed off the cream of the young men. These men I was teaching now were older, often married and sometimes with children, and they never quite knew how to treat me. It would be wrong to say they were all old enough to have been my father, but certainly they were often too old to be my contemporaries. And their attitude was one of deference because of the medals and the wound stripe I wore, the limp I'd acquired – and at times exaggerated a little for show – and the three years of active flying I had behind me. Yet it was also one of condescension because I was still not officially an adult and the moustache I'd grown to make myself look older only managed to make me look like a chicken with its first feathers – 'You've got some dirt on your lip,' Charley always said.

To be fair, sometimes I wasn't sure myself which category I fitted into – war hero or schoolboy. It was fun sometimes to talk of battle and strain and exhaustion but that was really just stretching a line, because, to tell the truth, after hospital I didn't feel in the slightest strained. I was young and resilient and I was full of life and itching to do the German air force more damage.

To my surprise, Charley was as good as her word and within three weeks of my arriving in Yorkshire I received a letter to say she was at the hospital at Harburton Bassett five miles away. I hadn't really thought she'd meant it but, when I rang the hospital to make sure, she answered breezily and when I arranged to meet her in Harrogate that Sunday afternoon, she turned up as bright as a button. Her cheeks were pink with the nippy Yorkshire air and, looking a picture in her uniform, she flung her arms round me with a shriek of pleasure.

'Told you I would,' she said.

'How did you manage it?' I asked.

'Easy. Told 'em my fiancé was stationed up here.'

My jaw dropped. 'Fiancé? Since when have you been engaged?'

'I'm not, ass!' She chuckled. 'I gave your name and all that, and they checked that you existed. After three years of war, they've learned to be considerate because they know that a girl always has to have a strong male breast to weep on from time to time.'

I grinned. 'You must be potty,' I said. 'Coming up to this draughty hole from the south.'

She gave me a funny look. 'Yes,' she said. 'I must.'

In between formation flying I did a little testing. No one knew much about testing at that stage but a chap called Roderic Hill had started asking himself questions and the business of test pilot was becoming more professional, so that occasionally I was asked to give my opinion on some new machine which arrived on the station. Most of them were awful and for the most part it was the same old nagging routine of showing ham-fisted pilots how to operate. None of them were keen to learn. They'd all read in the papers how people like Ball and Bishop and McCudden had gone alone into the skies in France to stalk the King's enemies – indeed, I'd tried it once or twice in the past myself – but times had changed since then, and we had to learn to fly in formation now. The old days of the lone wolves were over and no one could go anywhere these days without his friends tucked in behind him.

It wasn't 1917 any longer. It was 1918 and flying had changed. The war had become more ruthless and cold-blooded, and patrolling over the lines these days demanded professionalism, technical skill – and teamwork; and the day of the enthusiast had given way to the day of the expert.

The war in the air had never been anything to go into raptures about, of course, because people always got killed, but even so something had gone from it with the massed formations the Germans had started. No one went out alone or even in single flights any more. They went out stacked one squadron above another until sometimes you couldn't move for aeroplanes. 1914 had been the day of the rank amateur because no one knew a thing about war flying and 1915 hadn't been much better because even after a year of war we were only just beginning to develop the machines that could make air fighting possible. 1916 had been the year of discovery when we'd really learned how to set about one another and 1917 had been the year of the sky gods when the names of the experts had emerged on both sides of the line, men we'd all got to know and, if they were German, did our best to avoid.

There was still a lot to learn about 1918 but it was already becoming clear that the days of men like Ball were over. Ball was dead now and so was the Frenchman, Guynemer, and Voss, the German. Richthofen, my old enemy, was still around, with a score these days that was so high it seemed unbelievable; but he was being carefully guarded now by the German high command because his name alone was worth a couple of divisions, and he'd proved to be not immortal when he'd been wounded the previous summer. It had happened just before I'd met him after being taken prisoner, and perhaps he hadn't properly recovered then, because all I could remember of him was a small, blond man tired beyond his years, who looked as though he were badly in need of a long rest.

It was all these things that enabled me to accept the decision that I had to stay in England for a while. But the mind plays tricks and as the rest from the war did me good I began to forget what it had been like. Memory was always kind and I couldn't recall the grief and the sadness and the awful destruction in France, and could remember only the very real comradeship – something the newspaper writers who talked about it so glibly could never even begin to imagine – and the joy of serving with people like Ludo Sykes and Bull and Munro, now also in England like me. Frank Griffiths and Wickitt, who'd disappeared two years before over the Somme, never came back to trouble me these days and I'd even almost forgotten what my brother looked like.

And as I began to forget, I began to itch to go back. Several times I wrote to ask when I was going to be posted but the letters all went unanswered and in the end I even began to become aggressive and demanding, as though to go back to war was my right and privilege; finally the CO refused to countersign them.

'If I send that,' he said, throwing my latest angry epistle back across the desk at me, 'they'll demote me and probably send you to the Tower.'

The weather, which in Yorkshire was never of the easiest for flying, began to show some signs of improvement and I knew it wouldn't be long before the winter quiet ended and the war woke up again. And I wasn't far wrong because on March 21st, in a dense fog, the German offensive on the Somme broke over the Fifth Army. Men returning from the front brought stories that the high command and the government had been warned a dozen and one times of its approach. But the generals, it seemed, had failed to realize where it was going to fall while the government, after the slaughter of the Somme and Passchendaele, had starved the army of reserves in case the generals took it into their heads to have yet another go.

England was downcast at the news and, despite the nonsense that was written in the papers about strategic withdrawals, it was obvious a great deal of territory was being given up.

'We're right back where we were before 1916,' Charley said one Sunday afternoon as we walked alongside the river. 'The whole stupid war's gone into reverse.'

'Not for long,' I said. 'They'll never break through.'

'How do you know?'

'I just do.'

There was an aeroplane in the distance and I caught her eyes on me as I stared at it.

'Camel,' I said.

'How can you tell?'

'Sound of the engine. The way it hangs in the sky. That sort of thing.'

'I can hardly see it.'

'That just goes to show the superiority of men over girls.'

'Smug!' She frowned. 'Do you really think they'll stop the Germans, Martin?'

'Yes. Why? Are you worried?'

'Of course I'm worried! Lor', it would be so nice to think it'll all be over so I can go back to bein' featherbrained and stupid again and think of only clothes and dances and things, because sometimes, the way things are goin', I see myself runnin' up and down wards and corridors until I'm forty or fifty, gettin' a bit slower every year, until I finally grind to a stop. It gives me the jim-jams at times.'

'It'll not be like that,' I said. 'You'll see.'

As it happened, I was right. By the end of the month the German attack began to peter out and everyone began to look more cheerful, and the old hands coming back from France said that this time the Germans had over-reached themselves and were in trouble. Despite the gloom in the newspapers, I thought they might be right and began to worry that it would all be over before I got the chance of another go.

In a fret of anxiety I tried a few more tentative letters that brought no response. Then on April 1st, a rough, rainy day with no flying, the Royal Flying Corps became officially the Royal Air Force.

'Why?' Charley asked disconcertingly. 'What was wrong with the Royal Flying Corps?'

'The navy and the army keep on wanting to push us around,' I explained. 'Telling us what jobs we ought to do, that sort of thing. And, as anybody knows, generals and admirals don't know a thing about air power while there are quite a few fliers around now who think we should retain that right for ourselves.'

'My,' Charley said. 'Listen to the politics! Anyway, since it's happened, do you feel any different?'

'Not really. Funny they should pick April Fool's Day, though. Hope it isn't an omen.'

However it set me fretting again about going back to France, and finally, somewhere in the dim recesses of the corridors of authority, someone noticed my letters at last and eventually, just when I'd begun to think I was going to be training hamfisted pilots for ever, the posting came through.

The CO handed me the signal with a curious look on his face. 'France,' he said.

'Where?'

'Berck. Pilots' pool. You're to fly a new machine across.'

'What squadron am I going to?'

'I don't know.' He smiled and, standing up, reached for his cap. 'But, as it so happens, I'm just on my way to see the flight-sergeant about the state of serviceability, which will leave my office empty. I know it's forbidden to use service communications for private business but if I don't know about it, I can hardly be difficult, can I?'

He closed the door behind him and I stared after him, grinning like a clown, before snatching up the telephone. When I finally got in touch with Sykes' relative, he hooted with laughter.

'I've been expecting you to ring all morning,' he said.

'What squadron am I going to?' I demanded. 'What am I flying? Who's CO? Anybody I know?'

'Whoa! Whoa!' he said. 'I don't know any of those things.'

'Well, who does?'

'Nobody.'

'Nobody?'

'Well, nobody over here. I've done what I can and you'd be surprised how many strings I've had to pull. Be thankful that you're going at all.'

'When?'

'End of the week.'

'Is that all you can tell me?'

'That's all. Just get there. After that it's up to you. It's the best I could do but I seem to remember that you were never behind the door when low cunning was handed out.'

It seemed to me that I was being told to pick my own spot and I felt better at once. Snatching up my leather coat, an ancient one I'd had ever since 1915, which other pilots said they couldn't get within a yard of for the smell of castor oil, I went out for my last chore. One last trudge around the sky, I thought, and then it was over.

I got them off the ground in a ragged V and at 10,000 feet I felt I could see the whole of Yorkshire from the Pennines to the sea. Somewhere down below people were walking, talking and going about their dull daytime business while I, surely one of God's chosen few, was sitting high in the void of the sky, staring down at the blue-tinted plate of the earth aglow with sunshine, aware of the privilege of being different.

I was flying one of the new SEs with a Viper engine and it was as steady as a rock. What a wonderful firing platform it must be in action, I thought, and for the life of me, I couldn't think why they hadn't given it two Vickers guns shooting through the propeller, instead of one, with a Lewis on the top wing where you couldn't get at it.

This was a triviality, though, in the glow of pleasure I felt. The wing tips, ten feet away, blazed with the touch of the sun on the varnished fabric and I was caught by the amazing adventure of flight as if I were new to it instead of having partaken of it almost every day of my life for the last three years. There was nothing between me and the earth but a light linen-covered wooden structure and a two hundred-horse engine. The fabric of the lower wing was bellying slightly in the suction of the air stream passing across it and I could see the streamlined wires quivering in the vibration. In front of me was an array of instruments which made me shudder to think how few there'd been when I'd first flown, and about me was the faint whiff of petrol, dope, and hot metal and oil. I was hanging on nothing, high above the earth, my eyes full of sun and my heart full of the joy of flying. It was a fleeting glimpse of heaven.

I turned and saw the other machines just behind, moving up and down one after the other in currents of air like horses on a roundabout or a trot of boats in the lap of the sea, first one above me and then the other, the sun catching their varnished fabric and plywood fuselages and the helmeted heads of their pilots. We had two styles of formation flying: an open, fighting formation in which the machines were well apart with room to manoeuvre, the formation I favoured; and a prettier exhibition formation that the bigwigs who'd never flown in action fancied, in which the closer the machines could fly the better. The only value of this one that I could see was that it was good practice and in it formation turns had to be made carefully in case the machines fouled each other. In the more open formation, we'd worked out an about-turn which reversed the direction quicker than going round in a circle, and, while the leader did a half-roll on to his back, coming out directly below facing the opposite way, the machines on either side turned left and right about, crossing each other to retain their respective positions but going in the opposite direction. It was neat and we thought we were rather good at it.

In fact, I suppose we were but it demanded a modicum of alertness and the pilot of the machine just behind me on my right that morning, a man called Callender, couldn't have been paying attention in spite of the number of times I'd drummed it into them all that they must. Perhaps he'd had a heavy night the night before, perhaps his wife was ill, perhaps he'd got into debt, anything, but he certainly wasn't watching what he was doing. We had opened out and had plenty of room, and I signalled for the turn and gave them plenty of time to absorb it before I gave the signal to break. Then I started a half-roll, expecting them to do their stuff as we'd practised, but instead of making a tight bank, as he should have done, Callender tried to follow me over and the next moment he'd flown into my wing tip.

The first I knew of what was happening was hearing the crunch as his propeller chewed away at wood and fabric, then I found myself dropping out of the sky in an uneven jerky side-slipping motion with pieces of aeroplane falling off all round me. I was going down with no hope of controlling the fall, and I saw Callender's machine hurtle past me making a strange whistling noise like wind blowing through a hole. Then I noticed the fabric of my upper wing wrinkling and smoothing out as I slithered from side to side and knew that the whole structure was loose, with the wing tip flopping up and down and the aileron flapping loose. I'd automatically cut the engine and switched off the petrol but then, suddenly, I saw the wing tip simply fall off and, as the motion changed, over the nose I saw the land begin to turn round like a whirling green plate as I began to go down in a wild spinning movement. All round me there were loud flapping noises and the clattering of wires against struts. Somehow, yanking at the stick, I managed to slow the rate of descent but I was so low by now that the whirling trees had changed from blurred green to individual leaves, then I heard the crash of foliage and the cockpit seemed to be full of greenery and twigs and small branches.

The machine tore itself to pieces and I fell out and found myself dropping through branches towards the ground, hitting every one of them on the way, it seemed. Finally I fell clear and, dazed, stupefied and half-conscious, landed flat on my back on to the top of a well-clipped hawthorn hedge.

Fortunately there were no stakes to break my spine and it caught me and bounced me off into a field and I was still lying there trying to get my breath back when a car came hurtling across the grass.

'By God,' an awed voice said. 'You must be the only man in the world who's hit the ground from 10,000 feet and come out of it alive.'

Chapter 2

It seemed ages before I could stop shaking. They had lifted me on to an examination bench and I could hear it creaking under me as I shuddered.

'Think there's something wrong with me?' I asked.

The shuddering had started in the ambulance they'd put me in and had grown worse all the way to the hospital.

'Don't be silly!' It was Charley, of all people, who was attending me. 'It's a bit of shock, that's all.'

'What happened to Callender?' I demanded.

'Who's Callender?'

'The chap who flew into my wing tip.'

Charley's face changed and the smile disappeared at once.

'He was killed,' she said shortly.

I was still jerking about as if I were suffering from spasms of some sort. 'Isn't there anything you can do to stop this shaking?' I said.

'It's probably the plague.' She was coldly efficient but the smile came back. 'The usual, I think, is a cup of hot sweet tea, a blanket and a good sleep. You'll be as right as rain by tomorrow morning.'

'I've got to be,' I said.

'Why?'

'I'm going back to France at the week-end.'

She swung round, startled. Then her eyes grew hot. 'You never told me!'

'I haven't had the chance. I only learned an hour or two ago myself. I've got to go to Dover tomorrow.'

'Over my dead body,' she said.

I sat up but she put a hand on my chest and pushed me down again. Her face had become expressionless and it worried me a little.

'Look, Charley,' I said. 'Don't act the giddy goat! I've got orders!'

'They can wait a day or two!'

'No, they can't!'

'You're enough to demoralize the whole army nursing organization,' she said, losing her temper.

'You came within an inch of being killed this afternoon. Or hadn't you noticed?'

'Of course I've noticed,' I rapped. 'I'm the one who's got the black eye and the thorns sticking into his backside from that damn' hedge.'

She jabbed a thermometer at me. 'People with shock usually stay in bed till they get over it. That's what you'll do. The war can wait for twenty-four hours.'

'They've never put me to bed for twenty-four hours when I've crashed on other occasions,' I said.

'Then they should have.'

'We'd have lost the war long since if they put everybody to bed for twenty-four hours every time they hit the deck.'

'You're about as far from the war here as you can get,' she pointed out tartly. 'Open your mouth.'

She pushed the thermometer so far in, in her anger, I thought I'd choke.

'What happened to the bus?' I managed.

'It's in little pieces spread over most of Yorkshire as far as I can make out.'

'Oh, well,' I said, 'I shan't want it now, anyway. I'm picking up a new one and flying it across.'

She stared at me, frowning. 'You want to go back, don't you?' she said.

'Yes.'

'Isn't it dangerous enough for you here?'

I grinned. 'More. It's much safer with the Germans than with ham-fisted trainees. We call them "Huns", did you know?'

She looked down her nose at me. 'You're not the only ones with silly habits,' she said. 'We call the patients "Huns". I expect the reasoning's much the same. Why is it so important to go back?'

'Because there are people in France still fighting,' I said.

She shrugged, determined not to be coaxed down off her high horse. 'Even pugilists stop between rounds to draw breath,' she said.

She had the gift of reducing me occasionally to the point when I couldn't find an answer. There wasn't one this time. 'I'm sorry about Callender,' I said. 'He was a married man. With two children.'

'Three,' Charley said. 'Another one arrived this morning. They thought he'd survived and sent the telegram here. I saw it.'

The news shook me. 'That must have been what he was thinking about,' I said. 'He certainly wasn't thinking about flying.'

Charley removed the thermometer and looked at it critically. 'Normal,' she said. 'Unfortunately. How do you feel?'

'Fine now you've pulled out the thorns.'

'You sure?'

She looked at me critically and I grinned. 'Honest,' I said. But when I thought about it again I wasn't quite so sure. I'd had every kind of crash possible in my career as a pilot but I couldn't ever remember it affecting me like this. 'Except for the shakes,' I added.

'That could be tiredness,' Charley said.

'I've been in England for six months!'

'Courage's expendable, you know. Eventually you can use it all up——'

'I'm all right.'

'——and when you get to that stage, something big like this can start it off all over again. Perhaps I ought to keep an eye on you and go to France myself.'

'You?'

She grinned. 'Why not? They're askin' for volunteers. And it'll entitle me to wear a putty medal when the war's over.'

'Where'll you go?'

'There's a big hospital at Etaples and plenty of others nearer the fightin'. Where the nurses comfort the brave heroes as they're brought back bandaged and bloody.'

I knew she was getting in another of her sly digs at me, because she'd never been taken in by all the tales of gallantry and glory put across in the newspapers.

'Will they let you?' I asked.

'If I decide to go,' she said, 'just let 'em try to stop me.'

'I'll arrange to meet you,' I suggested. 'And dine you out in Amiens. Egg and chips. It's the permanent standby of the British army in France. It makes you wonder where the French got their reputation as cooks.'

'It's an idea,' she agreed. 'And you certainly need *someone* to keep an eye on you. I've never heard of anything so silly in my life! Fancy itching to get back into the fray while you're still in hospital.'

'I'm all right,' I insisted. 'Feel my pulse.'

'Not likely. I'm fed up with feeling your pulse. I think you're barmy.'

There was no one in the corridor so, grabbing her hand, I pulled her towards me and gave her a quick peck on the cheek.

'You must be feeling better,' she said dryly as she freed herself. 'You've never handed those around much before. Besides—' her face changed and she paused, fiddling with the thermometer and its case '—Ludo said there was another girl.'

The grin faded from my face. 'Yes,' I said. 'There was.'

'Do I know her?'

'Shouldn't think so.'

'What was her name?'

'Marie-Ange.'

'Marie- *what*?'

'Marie-Ange de Camaerts. She's a Belgian. She helped us escape.'

'Oh! That one!' Charley looked deflated and I knew what she was thinking. Marie-Ange was part of that life in France of which she knew nothing. She was the girl who'd risked everything – even her life – to help us get away and I'd promised I'd go back when the war was over and seek her out. I'd been a little in love with her, in fact, I think, chiefly because she was pretty and had a funny accent when she spoke English, but after several months I found now that I could barely remember what she looked like and, though I tried hard, it was growing more difficult every day to hold to my promise.

'What was she like, Martin?'

'About your age,' I said, 'perhaps a bit older. The family had lived behind the German lines ever since 1914. She brought food to me and Ludo and found us clothes and then she led us all the way from Noyelles near Tournai to Phalempon. She was going to take us to the coast. Walking all the way. All the way, Charley! But then we got this aeroplane, and we had to go. It was our chance and we had to take it. We never even managed to say goodbye to her. But if it hadn't been for her I'd still be a prisoner of war and so would Ludo. Ludo went back later and tried to drop a message at the farm where we hid but there was no one there. Perhaps the Germans came and took her away. Probably even shot her like they did Nurse Cavell.'

There was no smile on Charley's face. 'And this is why you have to go back?'

'Well, the war's bound to end eventually—'

'I've seen no sign of it.'

'Well, when it does I want to find her and thank her properly. I promised I would.'

She smiled and put the thermometer away at last. 'That's all right then,' she said. 'I thought it was something I'd done.'

'Oh, no,' I said earnestly. 'Nothing you've ever done, Charley. I just must know. That's all.'

She studied me. 'You know, Martin,' she said briskly. 'If it hadn't been Ludo that Jane married, I'd have said she wasn't right in the head to throw you over.'

Then she swept out of the ward before I could ask her what she meant.

Despite her good intentions, she didn't keep me in hospital and that week-end, as ordered, I flew to France, leaving from Dover and lining up on the two white markers they'd erected to give navigators a route across the narrowest part of the Channel. I landed at Clairmarais soon afterwards.

I got the shock of my life. I thought they'd be pleased to see me, that they might even know of me. But since I'd last been out, efficiency had taken over the army in France and things were different. Perhaps the failure of Passchendaele and Cambrai had set the government thinking that something was wrong with the direction of the war, because they'd given the command of all the allied troops on the continent to a Frenchman and put a businessman in charge of military transport. Everyone had suddenly become efficiency-conscious, so that the organization that had sprung up for the disposal of pilots along the front had become too intricate and vast to be true.

I'd expected to avoid all the nonsense of reporting to the pilots' pool at Berck for a posting. I'd felt sure that somebody would have heard that Captain Martin Falconer, DFC, MC (and one or two other insignificant French and Belgian decorations), was back, and since, young as he was, he was itching for action, would promptly take him on one side with an arm over his shoulder.

'What squadron do you fancy, old boy? Fifty-six is a good one. Sixty's not bad. Or how about Twenty-four?'

It wasn't a bit like that. The new system had got a stranglehold on France and they took the aeroplane from me without a word of thanks and sent me to

Berck in the next tender as if it were my first time out. And Berck turned out to be a sort of livestock depot where bodies were shunted up to the front or back to England according to need. There was no comfort and the camp staff were kept quite separate from the people who were going to do the fighting – in case they caught some disease from them, I supposed – while the pilots were treated like dirt. It was like being in an initial training camp again. The food was awful, and people of staff rank were bowed in and out of cars as though they were visiting royalty. Everybody seemed to drop on one knee to them and service at the front didn't seem to count at all.

As far as I could see, the people who were running the place were just organizing things for their own comfort, and mere captains like me were given only the slightest indication of respect, while lieutenants and second lieutenants were regarded as if they were something the cat had dragged in. It was an efficient barracks of a place with all the rigmarole like flagstaffs to hoist the ensign up and down in the morning and evening, and 'No Admittance' and 'Keep Out' and 'Staff Only' notices plastered everywhere. There were guards on every corner and miles of barbed wire, and dozens of other pilots besides me. The place was jammed with them, in fact, and after a quiet winter with few casualties the squadrons were making no demands. Most of the older men were content to wait their turn, happily aware that they might live longer that way, and some of them had been waiting for a matter of weeks, while it was quite obvious that all the time more were arriving than were ever leaving.

I'd been there three days, wondering what had happened to the war, with all the staff officers about the place making the most of their cushy posting and running the show as though it were a private dust-up of their own, indifferent to the men who were expected to do the dying. Then I had a passage of arms with a young staff captain, all red tabs and armband, who wore a pair of breeches that looked as though he'd been poured into them and field boots which had never been nearer a field than the path to that smart little office of his smelling of wax floor-polish.

There was a little triangular-shaped piece of wood on his desk with his name and rank on it. His rank was only the same as mine but his name was one I knew well because I'd read it in the society magazines like *The Tatler* and *The Sphere* and *Country Life* that found their way into the messes I'd used. He came out of the top drawer like Ludo Sykes and Charley but he was as different from them as chalk was from cheese. Their family had always considered that the privileges they enjoyed because of their wealth and rank made special calls on them and demanded special sacrifices. This little worm, who'd obviously got his job through influence, clearly felt that his caste gave him only privileges.

'I came out here to join a squadron,' I told him sharply when he argued.

'So have a lot of other chaps,' he said coldly.

'I've been waiting for six blasted months in England,' I went on. 'I'm sick of waiting.'

'Hard luck!' He stuck his nose in the air. 'You decorated boy wonders have to remember that people like me have other things to do besides just sort you out.'

I was so angry I jumped to my feet, and I think he thought I was going to hit him because he hurriedly pressed the button of a bell on his desk and a sergeant appeared while I was still glaring at him. He was as pale-faced and well-ironed as his captain but I suspected he'd seen this sort of thing before, because he opened the door wide for me.

'This way, sir,' he said quickly.

Outside, he gave me a look of sympathy but I was too angry by then to notice and literally smashed my way through the double doors at the end of the corridor. As they swung open, I felt them collide with someone who'd just been on the point of entering and heard a clatter, then a furious voice outside rose to a pitch of indignation as high as the top note of a set of bagpipes.

'F'r heaven's sake, ye bluidy fuil, watch whit ye're up tae!'

The man outside, a little knob of a human being no more than about five feet two with a face like a potato behind a bony beak of a nose and sandy hair that stood up on his head like a worn doormat, was literally dancing with rage. He was wearing a kilt and a bonnet and was holding his nose; two walking sticks were lying on the path by his feet.

'Ye've bust ma bluidy nose,' he was yelling. 'A mon would think this damned place was put up just tae gi'e wee whipper-snappers like you something tae do instead o' getting fellers tae the front—'

I was grinning all over my face, and as he finally turned, his hands lowered, to study me for the first time, the purple fury in his cheeks died and a grin as wide as my own spread across his features.

'Jock Munro,' I said.

'Brat Falconer!' His voice rose to a screech like a banshee's. 'The wee laddie himself!' And he leapt at me – or rather staggered, because he'd walked with sticks ever since he'd been wounded as an infantryman in 1915 – and clutched me in a bearlike hug.

His appearance had lifted my spirits at once. He'd been almost the first person I'd met when I'd reported to France in Bloody April of 1917 and it seemed like a good omen that he should be almost the first person I should meet in 1918. He seemed as pleased as I was.

'Mon, mon,' he was crooning in an accent that was thick enough to cut with a knife. 'It's gey guid tae see a familiar face again! Did they let you oot o' prison, then, tae win the war for 'em?'

'Well, they told me an old lag by the name of Munro was on his way over,' I retorted, 'and that he needed an assistant.'

'Mon, mon!' He seemed bereft of speech for a while, then a whole flood of reminiscences came tumbling out. 'Ye remember Rochy-le-Moutrou, an' the days when we were tryin' tae drive off the DVs with yon old Pups? An' the Bloody Red Baron an' the day they gave ye a bouquet for knocking doon a Hun because naebody had knocked one doon before?'

As he shouted the words we were doing a lumbering, tottering jig, watched by a startled staff major who was trying to get past, dancing first on one foot and then on the other in an attempt to slip through the door.

As we stopped, he stared at us. He was obviously expecting a salute, but instead we stared defiantly back at him and for a moment I thought he might put us on a charge for not acknowledging him. But then I saw his eye run along the ribbons under my wings and, as he decided that perhaps we were a pair of mad types who might well attack him if he said anything, he merely raised his stick to answer a salute he hadn't had and disappeared. Munro glared after him.

'This damned place's full o' yon types,' he snorted.

'I've met one or two,' I grinned.

'All hoity-toity. All Eton and Oxford. All wi' plums in their mooths so ye cannae understand whit they're sayin'.'

'I expect *they* had a bit of difficulty, too,' I said. 'I notice you still talk that barbaric language they speak north of the Forth.'

He sniffed. 'Finest Eenglish in the worrld spoken in Aberdeen.'

'It's a wonder they don't shove you in clink as a German spy. How long have you been here?'

He grinned at me. 'Five days, mon. The longest five days o' ma life.'

'I've been three. Why haven't I spotted you before?'

He chuckled. 'Because Ah've found a way oot through the wire, mon. An' there's a bonny little estaminet just doon the road. Eigg an' chips an' red wine. Awfu' cheap, too!'

It sounded dreadful but it was better than the camp.

'Let's go,' I said.

–

45

An hour later, full of egg, French fried, and *vin ordinaire rouge* so tart it tasted of iron filings, we began again to swop reminiscences.

'How's Sykes?' Munro asked.

'In Scotland,' I said. 'And married. Lieutenant-colonel now.'

'Mon, yon's travellin'. An' y'r leg?'

'All right. I limp a bit.'

'It shouldnae do ye much harm. *Ah* limp a lot. Ah haird that Latta was a lieutenant-colonel, too, now.'

Latta had been commanding officer of the first squadron we'd belonged to, a bull-headed pompous man whose idea of fighting a war was to send everyone on cross-country runs when the flying corps had been literally clawing itself into the air in inferior machines against Richthofen and his new Albatroses.

'That's right,' I said. 'At Hounslow.'

'Remember those two-seaters we brought down near Givenchy?' Munro said. 'And the Albatros? And yon time I flew a Fee intae the midden?'

'And that Gotha we got from Sutton's Farm?'

'We got the Camels we were praying for after ye went home,' Munro said. He wagged his head in admiration. 'Mon, yon's a pretty wee aeroplane.'

We continued to exchange memories for a while before coming back to Berck.

'Twenty fellers came in yesterday,' Munro pointed out. 'Six went oot. And, mon, the list's in a gey awfu' muddle. They're sendin' single-seater fellers tae heavy bombers an' heavy bomber pilots tae Camel squadrons.'

'There's no flying either,' I said.

'That's right. We've got tae get oot.'

'Where to?'

Munro grinned. 'Remember Bull?' he asked.

I nodded. Bull was another of the old squadron, a broad-shouldered, heavy-headed man of slow movement and smouldering temper.

'He's oot again. Near Bertangles. On SEs. Place called Pouleville. Ever flown SEs?'

'Not half. I've been flying 'em all round York-shire.'

'Same here round Scotland.' He beamed. 'Bullo's leading a flight. He suggested Ah join him. They're needin' a replacement.'

'Just one?'

47

'Och—' he gestured '—it willnae be long before they need another.'

'We'd never do it,' I said. 'You've no choice at this place.'

'No?' He leaned closer. 'There's one way, mon.'

That night, he commandeered the piano in the bar. It was out of tune and Munro couldn't really play, but he could bang out melodies for a sing-song and he got the whole miserable bored lot roaring.

> *'It's the only only way*
> *It's the only trick to play!'*

For the first time in months I felt I was home.

The next morning we went to the office to see if there were any news of postings. There were a lot of pilots hanging about – some young and brand new, others with the old wild look that Munro wore, who'd been out before, and a few old sweats who didn't care what happened – all giving particulars about themselves to be added to the sheets of names compiled by an overworked corporal clerk. As we strolled into the orderly room, Munro indicated the long lists of men requiring units, and the shorter ones of units requiring men, lying alongside a type-writer. The corporal clerk who had just made them out had his head in the cupboard looking for fresh papers and was in too big a hurry to attend to us. Munro had his pipe in his mouth and he tapped the list with his matches. His name was near the bottom. Mine was two above it. 'Enough names there, mon, tae staff a whole new flyin' corps,' he muttered. He looked indignantly up at the clerk. 'Ma name's a long way doon, corporal!'

The corporal turned and shrugged apologeti-cally. 'Some of 'em have been waiting a month, sir.'

'Is that a fact?'

As the corporal turned away again, Munro looked at me and struck a match to light his pipe. But, instead of applying it to the tobacco, he calmly touched it to the corner of the sheets of names instead.

I was ready and waiting. We'd worked out the moves carefully the night before in the bar. Giving Munro a violent shove that sent him cannoning against a desk to upset a whole pile of files on to the floor, I swung round as the paper he'd set alight flared into a flame and began to shout in a great show of panic.

'Och, ma God!' Munro yelled in horror, managing as he recovered to send another pile of papers flying.

'Look out, you fool,' I yelled. 'You'll set the whole place alight!'

In a moment the office was bedlam. As Munro backed away, his eyes wide with alarm, his mouth open yelling 'Fire!' the men waiting in the corridor, bored with hanging about, pushed their heads round the door and began to cheer and yell 'Encore!' and 'Bravo!' and 'Give the man a medal!' With great presence of mind, I snatched the sheet from the desk and threw it to the floor to stamp on it as hard as I could until the flames had gone. It was soon over except for the smell and the smoke and the ash on the floor, and the pilots disappeared again, one after the other, bored once more after the little interlude. But the corporal clerk was staring at the wreckage of his office and the crumpled list with horror.

'For God's sake – sir,' he said hoarsely, just managing to acknowledge that I was an officer and he wasn't, 'look what you've done!'

'There's gratitude for you!' Munro pushed forward officiously. 'Captain Falconer saved us all from gaein' up in flames, mon!'

Long-faced and horrified, the corporal couldn't have cared less. His precious lists were so well and truly marked by my boot — because I'd been careful to make sure they were — they were in no state to be presented to anyone in authority.

'Ma fault, corporal,' Munro explained calmly. 'Ma fault entirely. Ma match broke an' dropped on it.' He shook his head solemnly. 'Actually, mon, you're gey lucky. If it hadnae been for the captain ye'd ha'e lost the lot. Mebbe the whole office. Mebbe the whole building. Mebbe the whole camp even.'

The corporal stared gloomily at the crumpled list, unimpressed by the suggestion that he'd only just been saved from death by incineration.

'But it's for the CO — sir — and it's the only list I've got.' His eyes were still shocked. 'He'll never accept it like that. I'll have to do it all again, and I've another over there to do. In a quarter of an hour he'll be in screaming for it!'

'Och, mon!' Munro was all eagerness now. 'Yon's nae bother at all. Ah can type fine. Ah used tae work in the borough engineer's department in Aberdeen. Just gi'e us a wee bitty paper and ah'll type it for ye while Captain Falconer reads the names oot. Mebbe ye have anither machine ye can use while we use this one?'

The corporal looked as though he were going to burst into tears with gratitude and, while he disappeared to the next room to start work on another machine, Munro and I pulled up chairs. Munro rolled a new sheet of paper into the machine in front of him.

'List o' pilots,' he said, as he began to tap the keys. 'Pilots for single-seater fighters.' He typed about as well as he played the piano but with the aid of a rubber, he was doing quite well. 'Name, rank and number.' He turned to me. 'Noo, mon, fairst name.'

'Munro,' I said. 'Captain Hector Horatio.' I stared at him. 'I never knew you were called *that*, Jock.'

He shrugged, tapping away. 'It's somethin' ah try verra harrd tae keep dark,' he said. 'Next.'

'Falconer, Captain Martin.'

He grinned, tapped a few more words out then peered at what he'd done before sitting back with a deep sigh of satisfaction.

'Weel, weel,' he said. 'Just fancy that. If they havenae both been posted tae Captain Bull's squadron at Pouleville!'

Chapter 3

As it happened, Munro had got it a little wrong. Bull was in the Bertangles area all right, but his squadron was at Hizay not Pouleville, and instead of flying SEs they were flying Sopwith Camels. The news didn't worry us overmuch, however, because we'd both flown Camels before and liked them.

As the tender carried us south and east we passed along straight tree-lined roads where the hedgerows were white and dusty. There were dozens of lorries, ambulances and staff cars and I noticed that, though horses were still in evidence, it had clearly become a mechanical war since I'd last seen it. There were still farm carts on the roads, however, and peasants in blue smocks and sabots in the fields, and women standing at back doors. The place looked the same as it always had, and I couldn't believe it was six months since I'd been there. It was as though I'd left it only the day before and I decided that Berck was only an oasis that didn't really belong in the war at all.

The driver, like all drivers of Crossley tenders who ferried pilots about France, knew exactly where he was going and the location of every squadron in the area, no matter where it was tucked away up a country lane or behind a wood out of sight, and he expertly dropped the other pilots one by one along the road until there were only Munro and myself left.

Then, unexpectedly, we passed a large contingent of troops marching along the main road and, though soldiers were common enough after nearly four years of war, there was such an unusual quality of vigour in the stride of these men that we found ourselves turning to stare at them again.

They seemed taller than any soldiers I'd ever seen and I wondered if they were a new guards battalion because they were in marked contrast to the under-sized armies of pale-faced recruits that were being called up now. All that had been best and finest in mankind had rushed to the colours in 1914, full of patriotism and eagerness to do their bit, and the men who were now being conscripted contained types who wouldn't have been accepted then, many of them the stunted results of years of under-feeding in city slums. These men were different, and their uniforms seemed just too good and too well-fitting so that I wondered if they were officer-cadets or Australians or New Zealanders, because they moved with such excellent rhythm and such arrogant self-respect. But I'd got to know the Australians and New Zealanders only too well by that time, both groups turbulent and self-possessed, and even as it dawned on me who these well-disciplined men were the driver tossed aside his cigarette and cocked a thumb at them.

'Yanks,' he said.

They waved at us as we roared by and we grinned back at them – overjoyed to see them because we'd been expecting them for so long. These were the men who were going to save Europe from the Germans and bring the war to an end. I was delighted to see so many of them.

'Where've ye been?' Munro yelled.

We were so pleased to see them, we were in a state of enthusiastic confidence about the outcome of the war by the time we reached Hizay. We'd been waiting for them ever since the United States had joined the allies the previous year and, having seen them, having noted their strength and size and confidence, we felt able to sit back with the sure knowledge that the war was as good as won. It was only a matter of time.

It was all the more startling when we arrived to find Hizay full of gloom. The commanding officer was at Bertangles next door and there were long faces all round as the Crossley tender dropped us. At first I thought something had gone wrong with the war because, although the German advance had been slowed down, they were still trying to push forward and were making a mess of a lot of allied plans. Behind the lines, though, there had been a sureness that for once they'd overdone it and that the minute their attacks died away, the great sweep forward that would win the war would begin, so that I couldn't understand why everyone seemed so depressed.

It was only when Bull appeared, big and square, his large heavy head down between his shoulders as though about to rush at someone, that we learned what it was all about.

'They've got Richthofen,' he announced.

'Dead?' Munro said.

'Dead.'

'They never did!' Munro sounded shocked.

'Yes.' Bull seemed equally upset, as though something incredible and impossible had happened. 'This morning. Chap from 209 Squadron.'

'How do they know?' We were still sceptical.

'They've got his body,' Bull said. 'He was flying a red triplane and it came down near the Bray-Corbie road. There was the usual dust-up near Bertangles and a lot of machines flying round close to the ground. Some Australian machine-gunners claimed to have done it but they say it can only have been a Canadian called Brown. He did it from a naval Camel and they found the old Baron still sitting in the cockpit holding the controls. He must just have managed to slap her down before the candle went out. They dragged him away on a sheet of corrugated iron and they've got him lying in state now in a hangar at Bertangles.'

'Are they sure?' I asked.

Bull shrugged. 'Seems so,' he said. 'The machine's been pulled to pieces by now, of course – everybody grabbing bits for souvenirs and good luck charms – but they found an identity disc and a gold watch on him marked with his initials. Papers, too – one of them a pilot's certificate in the name of Manfred von Richthofen.'

It was easy to see why there were so many long faces. Richthofen's death probably meant life to dozens of young men on our side of the line, but it was still something that seemed to make the war different and uncomfortable and somehow I knew a turning point had been reached. Although he'd fought for the other side, we'd all known him so well he'd seemed almost like one of us. A little distant, perhaps, but one of us, nevertheless, so that his death had a saddening effect on us, as if the day had suddenly grown colder. Because we'd known and feared him so long, the fact that he could be killed set us thinking that the war must have reached a new and dangerous phase and it might well be our turn next.

'It started as a rumour,' Bull said, 'and it spread up and down the lines like wildfire. I thought the Hun was quiet today and when I got back I found out why. Some chap burst into the mess shouting "They've got the Bloody Red Baron". Perhaps the Germans were in mourning.'

'Well,' Munro said in matter-of-fact tones, 'Ah'm sorry for him o' course, but after all it's one less valley o' death tae ride intae.'

Bull laid on a tender and we all went over that afternoon. They'd cleared one of the flapping Bessoneau hangars and the body had been laid on a trestle-table dais, and when we arrived pilots, observers and ground crew were filing past, some merely out of curiosity, some to pay respect for a man who, whatever his nationality, had always been acknowledged as a great airman. There was no sense of triumph, though, and no jokes and a lot of men were even carrying wreaths and laying them on the growing pile round the bier.

I must have been the only man in that hangar who'd had the privilege of seeing Richthofen at close quarters, other than as a leather-capped head in an enemy machine in the air. When I'd made a forced landing behind the German lines I'd talked with him and he'd flattered me because I'd worn medal ribbons, and I'd even spent the evening with his *staffel* who'd wined and dined me before sending me off into captivity. Having seen him alive, it was stranger still for me to see him lying there dead. He was half-smiling, his nose and jaw injured in the landing, and he seemed even smaller than I remembered him, so that I felt an intense wave of pity as I looked at him.

Later that afternoon in the sunshine, with the light already changing to gold, six pilots of equal rank to Richthofen's carried the black-stained coffin to an open army tender, and, headed by twelve Australian infantrymen with their rifles reversed, the cortège passed slowly down the main street of Bertangles beside the aerodrome. Machines were landing and taking off all the time over the grave, which had been dug in Bertangles cemetery near a hemlock tree, and the place was full of allied soldiers, Chinese labourers and a few French women and children who were clearly wondering what all the fuss was about over one of the hated Germans. As the volley rang out over the grave the pigeons burst from the trees with a clattering lift of wings over the headstone, a cross made from an old four-bladed propeller. Somebody had attached a round plate at the centre with the words 'Cavalry Captain Manfred von Richthofen, aged twenty-two,' which as it happened was wrong, because according to what I'd been told when I'd met him, he must have been twenty-seven or twenty-eight.

Not that it mattered, anyway, because someone stole the plate soon afterwards as a souvenir.

The next day someone flew over the lines to drop a photograph of the grave and a note to the Germans to say he was dead and had been buried with military honours. A few people in England objected to the fuss, claiming that Richthofen was only a German, after all, but flying men knew what it was all about. Richthofen had been a flyer and that had put him apart, because the war, despite its new ruthless code, still somehow in the air managed to retain a few traces of dignity. In the sky, the battlefield wasn't the same sad waste of mud and wreckage it was on the ground. Up there it was swept clean after every fight and to the pilots filing past the grave, Richthofen was just a young man whose death was rousing the emotions they'd have felt for one of their own comrades.

As we drove back, to my surprise Bull began to quote John Donne – the only bit of Donne I ever knew, in fact. '*Any man's death diminishes me,*' he said, '*because I am involved in Mankinde; and therefore never send to know for whom the bell tolls; it tolls for thee.*' Munro gave him an odd look, as though, he, too, had never suspected Bull capable of emotion. 'Aye,' he said. 'Aye. That's aboot it.'

—

The major was a man with a DSO and an MC and several foreign decorations. Before the war he'd been a history scholar at Oxford but had rushed to join the artillery without taking his degree. He'd soon transferred to the RFC and he'd done so well he'd decided not to go back to Oxford, because if the navy and the army allowed the new RAF to survive — which at that moment still seemed very unlikely — he was set for a rapid climb to seniority. He was a burly man with a heavy jaw, a sharp tongue when anyone showed any sign of moral disintegration after a disaster, and a quiet sureness about him that appealed to me.

'You'll take over "A" flight,' he said, 'as senior flight commander. Munro will have "B". Bull's already got "C". It'll take a bit of doing for us to get used to two new flight commanders at once but I expect we'll manage it and I've heard a lot about you.' He smiled. 'As a matter of fact, I didn't think you were quite so young.'

'Perhaps we're all a bit young these days, sir,' I suggested and he nodded and lit a cigarette.

'Yes,' he agreed. 'I think we've all grown a little old before our time.' He gestured. 'You'll find things different these days. We tend to go out all together now. Richthofen started it with his big formations and we've had to follow suit. And until today his lot were doing very well. I think the chap you're relieving's glad to be out of it. That's why the mess is so noisy tonight. I'm letting Bull lead tomorrow, of course. Normally it would be your job but I think it'll do no harm to give you the chance to find your feet.'

Bull didn't seem to be looking forward to the job. He was low in spirits as though the episode in the hangar at Bertangles had affected him. 'The fun's gone out of the war,' he said heavily.

'I never noticed there was much hilarious aboot it,' Munro said.

'No,' Bull agreed. 'But something's gone. It's grown too big for individuals like us.'

'Aye,' Munro agreed. 'It showed at Berck.'

Bull managed a twisted grin. 'I suppose that sort of thing's what'll win it in the end,' he admitted. 'But they've taken something away, too.'

He was still puzzled about how we had *both* managed to get posted to the squadron and explained what had happened. 'We only needed one flight commander until yesterday,' he said. 'We lost another last evening. Chap called Brady. He wasn't popular with his last mob and even his best friend couldn't have called him a thruster, and when the Old Man detailed him to lead a low raid on the aerodrome at Verq this morning he said he couldn't do it. The CO told him it could mean a court martial, so he shot himself – behind the mess in the middle of the night.' Bull shook his head. 'Seems funny that a chap has the guts to kill himself but not to take a chance which might have come off and brought him a gong.'

Munro shrugged. 'It isnae so funny tae me,' he said. 'I've often felt like it masel'.' He tapped the new ribbon the King had pinned on my chest. 'Ye see that, Bullo, and ye ken what ye have tae do tae get 'em?' He turned away. 'As far as ah'm concerned, Bratty can keep it.'

Bull nodded. 'You've only to stay alive to get 'em these days,' he grinned. 'Especially now the thing to do is trench-strafing. It smashed up the German counter-attacks after Cambrai and they're trying to work it now so that nothing on the German side of the lines will dare move after daylight. We spend most of our time these days below 1000 feet shooting at anything that moves.'

'Charming!' Munro said. 'Bluidy charming!'

'They think so much of it, in fact,' Bull went on, 'they're turning out a special aeroplane for the job. Salamanders. With extra armour. They're even training ground-strafing squadrons.'

'Aye,' Munro said. 'It's a gey fine idea, mon, but I'm pleased *I'm* no' in one.'

'Except,' Bull said with another grin, 'that when the fun starts they set *everybody* at it and then you might well end up wishing you were.'

–

Orders came through at dinner that the squadron was to move north to Puy in Flanders the next day and, imagining it was to be a period of rest away from the fighting in the south, the mess combined the celebration with the send-off for the time-expired man I'd relieved and threw a lunatic party. It was clearly a well run squadron and the major had been careful to make sure that among his fitters and riggers and drivers and clerks there were men who could play instruments. The war seemed to wake up as they tried to lift the roof. It wasn't anything patriotic like *God Save The King* or *Land of Hope and Glory* that they played but *Dark Town Strutters' Ball* and all the latest hits from London, and Munro sat back and beamed at them. 'Mon,' he said. 'Yon was a great idea the Major had.'

Bull laughed. 'Except that a few of the people we got rid of complained that he swopped them for a trumpeter and a packet of fags.'

As the band blared on, a low roll of engines started above us and Bull looked up. Above the muttering I could hear distant explosions, then there was a tremendous crash that seemed to lift my feet from the floor. The hut fittings shook and a shower of dust fell from the cracks in the roof.

'What's yon?' Munro demanded.

Bull looked up. 'Jerry bombers. Big ones. They come over every night these days. Ever since we formed the independent air force to raid Germany, they've been trying to get a bit of their own back. They don't hit much but it makes sleep a bit more difficult.'

Munro frowned. 'Noo I know the war's taken a turrn for the worrse,' he said.

'Half-past five, sir,' the batman said as he shook me. 'Leave the ground at half-past six.'

I sat up and, staggering half-blind with sleep to the corner of the hut, began to splash water on my face.

Munro lifted his head. 'What are ye washing for?' he demanded.

'Because I'm not a scruffy pig like you,' I said.

He climbed out of his sleeping bag. 'Ah dunno why ye bother,' he observed. 'Camels spray oil like a shower, and if ye fire y'r guns the muck all sticks tae it. Half an hour from now, forbye, ye might be deid. It's better to tak' y'r bath when ye land – *if* ye land.'

The mess was full of bleary-eyed men clutching leather coats, flying suits, scarves, goggles and helmets. The cook had gone mad and there were sausages, bacon and fried eggs that looked like great sad yellow eyes and were as hard to cut as rubber. Munro peered at his as though he were disappointed it didn't contain a chicken. 'Ma eigg's harrd,' he complained. He looked up at the mess servant. 'Mon, why are they *always* harrd. Boiled, fried, baked, roasted, poached or scrambled, they always end up feeling like a brick in y'r stomach when ye get up there.'

We trudged silently across the field, wrapping scarves round our necks and fastening belts and buckles and buttons in the faint steely light that was beginning to show huts and farm buildings. As we climbed into the machines, mechanics began to swing their legs and lean on the blades of the propellers, and engines began to cough into life with bursts of blue castor oil smoke.

Cold air slapped me in the face then the machines began to jolt with rocking wings across the grass behind Bull. As I pulled back on the stick the Camel lifted off the ground like a chained typhoon, and I gave it just a shade of left rudder to counter the engine's pull to the right. As it went up my heart went with it. The Camel was the sort of aeroplane I'd prayed for all through the war. It was a fighting aeroplane not a cart with wings such as we'd had to fly for so many years. It was unstable, tail-heavy and so light on the controls the slightest jerk could hurl it all over the sky. Difficult to land and fly in formation, it flicked on to its back like a bat, but in a fight its vices became virtues because it was also difficult to hit. It suited me far more even than the docile SE5 that all the big-scoring boys seemed to prefer, and I could only assume it was because its awkwardness went somehow with my temperament.

Below us the ground seemed dead and remote with just an occasional lifting column of smoke to indicate that anyone was alive down there, then the sun began to catch the leading edges of the wings as it peeped over the horizon and touched the tops of trees with gold. Dew-wet roofs flared with light, then, as it flooded across the flat Flanders fields, I could see the roads were full of guns and lorries all moving east.

For the first time the war seemed to be going well for the allies. The German offensive had only lengthened their line instead of shortening it and, as we'd seen, the Americans were arriving now to take a share of the fighting, tall straight men in strange breeches and gaiters, strong young men who were fresh to battle and actually looking forward to it and had none of the war weariness of the other embattled nations.

There had always been Americans around, of course, men who'd joined the French *Armée de l'Air* or the Flying Corps, and there'd even been a few of them at Berck, noisy light-hearted men always game for tomfoolery, who were awaiting a transfer to their own youthful air force.

'A fortnight from now,' one of them had said, 'we'll be jangling all over with medals. In our mob they give 'em to you three at a time, just for saying sweet nothings to the guy in command. And why not? It's good publicity. You guys need to wake up. I bet you printed the news of Waterloo on an inside page.'

It was a pleasant thought to feel there were so many of them coming. There'd been a lot of talk by their politicians about how they intended to darken the skies of France with the machines they were going to build but something had gone wrong there somewhere and the squadrons they were forming were all still being equipped with British and French aeroplanes. All the same, it was nice to think they were on our side instead of the other one and I was more than willing to move over a little to let them get at the Germans.

The sky was busy with aeroplanes and it was a cold morning with a strong wind and ragged clouds. We were soon over Arras which was still recognizable as a town, but only just, and the sun thrust a shaft of light dimly through the huddle of cumulus to the east so that it became possible to see the Bapaume road heading north and south. A few more clouds, the forerunners of an army, were moving up below and it was clear that before the day was out the sky would be completely shut in.

Bull didn't take any chances. It was his job to lead the squadron to Puy and, although he was supposed to be flying an offensive patrol, taking off from Hizay and landing at Puy, it was more important to get everyone safely to their destination than to be particularly offensive. Sitting well behind him, I was enjoying myself. Someone else was bearing the responsibility for a change and all I had to do was follow. As I stared about me, it struck me as surprising that only a year or two before I'd not considered myself particularly skilful even at main-taining a push bike and here I was, not yet twenty, and I had mastered several aero engines and several guns, photography, the Morse code, aerodynamics, bombs, the structure and rigging of aeroplanes and the interrupter gear that enabled me to fire through the propeller. And on top of this, because I'd always been a good shot, I'd acquired a reputation as a daredevil I didn't really deserve which came chiefly from the fact that I'd managed to survive and learn the tricks.

A loud double cough made me jump. Anti-aircraft fire always startled me at first, and I decided that if I flew in battle for the rest of my life I'd always jump at the first bang and the first sudden puff of black smoke.

The fifteen drab machines rose and fell about me as we rushed between the increasing murk. More clouds from the north were sweeping down like galleons with grey sails, threatening and filled with purple valleys and icy pinnacles. As they closed in, the glimpses of the hedgerows grew more fragmentary. The trenches lay on my right, a great grim wound stretching to Switzerland from the sea, with all the wreckage of war contained in a long winding strip of churned-up, stale, stinking ground bounded by trenches and barbed wire.

As the clouds grew thicker Bull climbed, picking his way between the misty towers, and suddenly for no special reason I could explain, I began to grow nervous. It was nothing that Bull was doing wrong, just a sort of prickling of the hair on the back of my neck, as some sixth sense that came from three years of flying made me know something was not as it should be. My eyes began to wander about the sky behind us, above and below, looking for the slow-shifting specks that meant death.

Eventually I spotted a group of half a dozen Albatroses just below and as I did so Bull saw them, too, and fired a Very light to draw attention to them. I found that my breathing was coming faster and the old familiar hollowness that always came before a fight appeared in my stomach. I shifted in my seat, settling myself, almost, for the coming battle. I could see the black crosses on the machines below now and Bull was clearly intending to attack. The Albatroses were on his route to Puy and there was no reason in the world why he shouldn't.

Except—

Just at that moment, as the aeroplanes fell like stones from the sky and the ground raced up towards us, from the corner of my eye I caught a glimpse of another group of specks against the clouds and I waved my arm wildly and pulled my flight out of the dive towards the right. Almost immediately, a dozen aeroplanes flashed past us, mixed Albatroses and Triplanes, in all the old red paint and gaudy colours that were so familiar.

As they shot down behind Bull and Munro we went after them, my heart thudding in my chest. Bull reached the Albatroses below and they wheeled and scattered like pigeons frightened in a wood by a gunshot, then one of them dropped out of the sky, streaming smoke. Tracers criss-crossed the battle area, then I saw the brightly-coloured machines crash in behind Munro. A Camel went twisting down before we joined in on their tails, then the size of the battle began to draw in other aeroplanes and I saw a squadron of SEs smash through the middle of the mêlée, and then a new flight of Albatroses and yet another, until the sky seemed to be full of machines. Ruddering wildly, I saw a Camel bearing Munro's big 'W' chased by an Albatros which was chased in its turn by an SE and then a Triplane, and I joined on the end of the ring-a-roses. As I fired, the Triplane fell apart into a floating wreckage of wood and canvas that shot past my wing tips, but as it did so I saw the SE roll over, too, and one of its wings fall off, so that it followed down in a flat spiral behind the stripped fuselage of the Triplane which was going down now like the stick from a spent rocket, its tail wagging slightly from its speed as it fell.

The Albatros behind Munro had sheered off in alarm but there was no time to watch it because I was facing another Albatros now and I could see the winking flashes from its guns and saw fragments leap from the Camel's centre section. If I turned away I'd present a perfect target so I did the only thing I could and kept on, straight towards a head-on crash, my heart in my mouth and praying the Albatros would turn. It did and as it lifted, it presented its belly to me and I saw the tracers striking it, then it dropped away, its tail almost touching my wing tip, fell into a fluttering spin, turned over on its back and dropped towards the clouds.

The fight was over as suddenly as it had started. The Germans vanished eastwards with the SEs after them, and the rest of us were trying to form up behind Bull again. We landed in ones and twos at Puy to count noses. The squadron lorries had just arrived and the mechanics were there waiting for us to land.

Munro jumped from his machine as soon as it rolled to a stop and lolloped towards me in his flying boots to clutch me in a highly dramatic show of gratitude.

'Mon, just state y'r terms!' he said. 'Ah'll mak' over ma whisky ration and gi'e ye all ma estates roond Aberdeen. If it hadnae been f'r you, I'd no' ha'e been here the noo!'

There were three machines missing but, even as we were making out our reports, news came in that one of them, a youngster called Milne, had forced-landed without damage in a field, while a second, a boy called Walters, although he'd crashed, had walked away with nothing worse than a cut lip.

'There's one thing we can be certain aboot,' Munro said grimly. 'In spite o' the death o' the proprietor, the Richthofen circus hasnae gone oot o' business.'

Chapter 4

The new airfield was a bleak place without a tree or a bush for miles, and the squadron we'd relieved had removed all the furniture so that we had to settle into comfortless huts and a mess devoid of chairs. It didn't help that it was still bitterly cold in the evenings, and that mist crept from the river bottoms to fill the huts with its smoky smell and lay in the shallow folds across the field, so that at dawn the aeroplanes seemed to float without wheels on a sea of grey vapour.

The mess fire wouldn't have warmed a rat and, with a perpetual hunt for fuel going on, to quieten the grumblers someone had the bright idea of organizing a raid on a coal dump nearby which belonged to the Engineers. Though it would hardly have done for a senior captain like Munro to be involved in a subalterns' prank, he found it impossible to keep out and, as most of the squadron were young enough to be only just out of school, there was no shortage of helpers. He also roped in the flight-sergeant and the sergeant in charge of transport who lent a lorry. 'Providing, sir,' the flight-sergeant said firmly, 'that our names are kept well out of it and that *we* can have some of the coal.'

Munro grinned. 'Done,' he said. 'This isnae the army or the navy. This is a technical outfit, no' a lot o' stuffy old curmudgeons clingin' tae tradition.'

He had the bright idea of dressing everyone in kilts – 'Tae hide identities,' he said – and handed out to the men taking part what looked like skirts made out of blankets.

'Kilts,' he said. 'Hodden grey. London Scottish mebbe.'

There were still not many in the mess who wore even the RFC tunic and cap. Most still wore regimental uniform with wings except for a few like me who hadn't served as an officer in any other branch of the forces and wore the universal tunic with RFC badges. It made for a queer mixture of dress so that there was really no uniform at all and, since no allowance had been made for the new RAF outfit, which was said to have been designed by an admiral and a ballet dancer and was generally disliked as being too flashy, most of us just continued to wear RFC wings on an oily, stained jacket edged with leather. The 'kilts' at least gave us a uniform aspect.

'Bear in mind I'm not taking my bags off, though,' Milne pointed out.

'Ye cannae wear breeks wi' a kilt, mon,' Munro said scornfully. 'Ye'll look like an auld lady whose combinations ha'e slipped.'

'All the same—'

'Och, whisht!' Munro grinned. 'You Sassenachs! When the fiery cross went roond, the Highlanders used tae run through the snow wi' nothin' on but a plaid an' a dirk.'

'I bet it was chilly,' I said.

'An' we're *no'* Heelanders, forbye,' Milne said, imitating Munro's accent.

Munro's lip wrinkled. 'Ah can see that,' he said. 'An' thank God for it, too.'

In the end he compromised, provided everyone wore football stockings over boots to look like a Highland regiment's spats, then he jammed everyone's side caps top-dead-centre down over their heads and stuck tufts of feathers he'd scrounged from a nearby farm behind the badges to represent hackles.

Milne stared at himself in the mirror. 'I think I resemble either Abdul the Damned or the Monarch of the Glen,' he grinned. 'And this hat looks like a coffin for a cat.'

With a few of the brighter sparks pinning hand-kerchieves in front like sporrans, Munro announced himself satisfied and we set off just after dark. Munro, wearing his own kilt, and I – half-frozen in one belonging to a subaltern called Taylor who'd transferred from the Gordons – got the sentry on the dump talking, while the rest disappeared round the back to hump bags of coal into the flight–sergeant's lorry. Inevitably, as they finished, someone grew suspicious and the alarm was raised. There were yells of fury as they drove off and Munro and I took the opportunity to vanish into the darkness. They never came to the aerodrome but they clearly had their suspicions about the culprits and, as we gleefully hugged the huge fires we built, we heard there was a blazing row going on between the colonel of the Engineers and the indig-nant commanding officer of a battalion of Argylls resting in the vicinity.

'Yon kilted rogues,' Munro said severely. 'Ye cannae trust 'em anywhere!'

For three days, the weather was so bad there was no flying at all, and looking at the map it occurred to me that as the crow flew I was now only a matter of thirty-odd miles from Noyelles where I'd first met Marie-Ange. The last sight I'd had of her as we'd lifted the stolen Albatros from the aerodrome at Phalempon was of a small figure heading south with just the flutter of a white handkerchief to indicate that she knew we'd seen her. With two of us in a cockpit built for one and three German aeroplanes after us, there hadn't been much we could do about waving back, and that picture of the fluttering handkerchief was all I had. It would never go away as long as I lived, and again and again I found myself wondering what had happened to her. When it came to occupying a country, the Germans didn't play games and there would inevitably have been an enquiry into where we'd hidden after escaping, so that I just hoped they'd made their enquiries round Phalempon and not at Noyelles where we'd first run into her.

I was still wondering about her when, on the last of the three dud flying days, a letter arrived from Charley.

'I'm coming to France,' she said. 'I've been posted to the hospital at St Marion.'

It sounded like a breath of fresh air and I suddenly realized I'd been waiting for it ever since I'd arrived.

The front was reasonably quiet now that the German attacks had died down and, with the death of Richthofen, some of the stuffing seemed to have leaked out of the German pilots. It had always been German policy to concentrate their best men into special squadrons, which meant that the others were never very good and, with the Richthofen circus, after that one encounter we'd had, apparently lying low, we all began to feel that life wasn't as bad as we'd thought it was. It was even said to be improving for the poor devils in the trenches, because the Germans were clearly wearing themselves out with their own offensives, just as we had on the Somme and Passchendaele and the French had on the Chemin-des-Dames.

Across the field was a Bristol squadron. Their two-seaters were strong and fast and they'd added all sorts of adaptions, alterations and refinements to them. They allowed me to fly one with Munro as observer and it was a joy to be in it. With a two hundred-horse Rolls Royce engine it could turn on a sixpence and, remembering those awful BEs I'd flown in 1916 when it was almost impossible to communicate with the observer, I was delighted to find that in the Bristol the two cockpits were close enough to shout into Munro's ear. The machine had had a bad start because it had been wrongly used at first and Leefe-Robinson, who'd got the VC for destroying the Zeppelin at Cuffley in Middlesex, had been taken prisoner after being shot down in one. The crews had got the hang of them now, though, and used them as fighters, the only difference being that they had a very useful gun firing rearwards to protect their tail and one or two crews were actually getting scores like Camel and SE pilots.

Patrols became humdrum, however, because it was growing difficult to persuade the Germans to accept battle and most of our time was spent manoeuvring into position or chasing them back over their own lines, and the squadron was unable to chalk up any more victories until May. By this time there was talk about a new Fokker coming out and the odd people who claimed to have seen one said they were very good, though I was inclined to suspect that a lot of the talk was just hot air because I didn't think any of them had reached the front yet.

Bull seemed to know all about them, though. 'They say it'll run rings round us when it arrives,' he insisted. 'And the only thing you can do is dive and zoom because they can out-waltz and out-fly us any time. They're supposed to be so good every Albatros works in Germany's making 'em.'

'Pairsonal information, Ah suppose?' Munro grinned. 'From the Kaiser himself?'

'It gets around,' Bull explained. 'Mercedes engines. One hundred and sixty-horse. Top speed about one hundred and twenty. Made of welded steel tubing covered with fabric. Light, nippy and fast.'

'You seen one?' I asked.

'Not yet. But they say they're all going to the best squadrons and they sit up high waiting to pounce on us.'

'Mebbe we'll be lucky,' Munro said. 'Mebbe they won't get a chance because we've left all the fighting away down in the south.'

Bull managed a twisted grin. 'For the time being,' he said. 'But the story's going round that we're only waiting for Jerry's offensive to die down and then we're going to hit him with everything we've got – everywhere.'

'Ah expect ye're right,' Munro agreed gloomily. 'It's usually ma luck tae arrive just in time for the offensive.'

—

For a while, however, it certainly seemed as if we'd left the fighting behind us. We saw none of the new Fokkers and, with most of the planes we met still Albatroses and Triplanes, there were no casualties. Life became quite humdrum, in fact, with regular high patrols, all of them producing nothing, not even a brush with the Germans, because they invariably disappeared as soon as they saw us. A few of the new pilots who were itching to show what they could do began to grow bored and eager for action, but the older hands like myself and Munro and Bull – even Milne and Walters, who had viewed the Germans' guns from the wrong end and had had to walk home for their trouble – preferred things as they were. We were none of us glory-seekers and we enjoyed being alive, and I for one always hated the business of the empty chair at dinner in the mess after we'd run into trouble. It was always studiously ignored, with the conversation louder and more inconsequential than normal in an effort to pretend it didn't exist, but I'd never once really acquired the knack of rubbing people from my memory as quickly as all that, and I never failed to see the late occupant sitting there as I'd seen him the night before or even at lunch that day.

Then, with the end of the month, the Germans seemed to wake up. Suddenly they began to appear in bunches, but the ones opposite us weren't very good or were badly led and made nothing more than darting attacks at us before bolting for home. Before May was more than a few hours old, however, I managed to surprise a group of them over Armentières and the would-be warriors among us had more than their fill of fighting.

The Tripes were always queer-looking machines and it was said that even Richthofen, who'd flown one regularly, had been none too keen on them and had continued to fly his Albatros when he could. But they were certainly nippy, could turn on a thumbnail and went up like lifts. On the whole, the Germans were still avoiding battle but this time they couldn't get away and I got one in my Aldis and gave it a long burst. It immediately reared up in front of me in an upward roll but, being heavy-tailed, the Camel was good at climbing too, and I went up after it and got in another burst as it levelled off. I didn't think at first I'd hit it but it suddenly flopped over into a spin and, deciding I'd put the wind up the pilot, I dived after him. Because we were equal in numbers and the other Triplanes were busy, it seemed safe to follow him down.

The Triplane was spinning like fury by this time, as though the engine was full on, and I had to drop like a stone to keep anywhere near it. I chased it down to 3000 feet when it spun into a cloud and I couldn't tell whether it crashed or whether the pilot had merely crept home with his heart in his mouth as I'd done myself more than once in the past.

As I climbed back again, the sky seemed to have emptied of all but three aeroplanes, a Triplane and two Camels. The Triplane seemed almost to be having the best of the exchanges, turning in a very small circle and firing every time its nose was pointing anywhere near one of the Camels. But the pilot was afraid to come out of his turn and the fight was drifting towards the lines, so I held the Camel's nose high and at eighty miles an hour it was vibrating wickedly as I forced it upwards.

As I came within range, I tried a burst. The pilot of the Triplane seemed startled at the advent of a new opponent and dropped in a twisting dive, pulled up in a tremendous zoom then fell over on one wing in a tight curving dive. He had managed to throw the other two Camels off-balance by the manoeuvre and they were caught wrong-footed, heading in the wrong direction, but, perhaps because he hadn't seen where the bullets had come from, his dive brought him close to me and I got in a full deflection shot as he whirled past. I saw the pilot's head turn in my direction then the Triplane dropped in another spin and I was able to follow it down, taking snap-shots at it as it went. It looked like being just like the last one but suddenly it crumpled with a sudden flop, the wings tearing away and fluttering in the air while the body fell sheer, dropping at a speed that took my breath away.

There would be no need to dig a grave for the pilot and it left me feeling a little sick.

As though to try to get some of their own back, the German Archie started blackening the sky with malicious puffs of smoke as we turned for home. For once the shooting was good and I felt the Camel lift beneath me but, without attempting to regain formation, we twisted and turned for the lines, heading for the drifting puffs on the understanding that no two shells ever burst in the same place.

As we crossed the lines, I was pleased to see that the other four machines were all behind me, picking up formation, and when we landed, everybody was all smiles, so that I knew the victory had done them good. Milne, who'd crash-landed after the last big fight, had crept about for days as though he were ashamed of what he'd done, but now he was jumping and dancing about with Taylor, grinning all over his face and slapping backs as though he'd defeated the whole German Air Force on his own. We all decided that Triplanes were revolting machines to look at and probably worse to fly, and that it was a startling sight to see all three storeys stand up and whirl away.

'But they break up,' Milne said solemnly, clicking his fingers. 'Just like that! One minute it was there and the next it was just a fluttering jumble of canvas and sticks like a broken kite. And, my word, the way that fuselage went down! Those pilots couldn't have been very good.'

When we exchanged news it turned out that, in addition to the one I'd broken up, Milne and Taylor had driven another one down, and soon afterwards the artillery rang up to say that a third had dived into the ground with full engine on just in front of them at the exact spot where I'd sent the first one down.

'Two in one fight, laddie,' Munro said enviously. 'What it is tae fly like a sparrow after a midge.'

The weather began to improve and with the numbers of British aeroplanes over the lines increasing all the time, it was pleasant for a change to feel fairly safe. At long last we seemed to have the measure of the Germans and, unless their new Fokker proved as wonderful as it was said to be, I felt life was going to be considerably rosier for us all, because their industry was said to be suffering from a shortage of materials by this time and they were all supposed to be drinking coffee made of ground hazelnuts.

Suddenly for the first time I really began to think the war was going to end. When it had started in 1914, I'd been terrified it would all be over before I got to the fighting, but then as 1914 and 1915 had given way to 1916 and 1917 I'd begun to feel it would *never* end. Men had come and gone so that I found now I couldn't even remember their names and they went past in the memory like ghosts. Ghosts remembered not for their skill as pilots but because they'd eaten a lot or drunk a lot or been good at playing chess. But now the vast dark tunnel we'd all been going through for so long suddenly seemed to have a spot of light at the end of it. Only a spot still because the tunnel was a long one, but at last there seemed hope that eventually we'd reach the end of it.

And not before time either, because they were scraping the bottom of the barrel at home by now and had pushed up the military age to fifty-one – though all it seemed to do was reduce industrial efficiency rather than increase military power – and, of course, Russia was out of the war. But it was being said now that the revolution there was beginning to have its effect in Germany too, and that the people in Berlin were talking of strikes – a very different thing from when they'd marched into Belgium at the beginning of the war, so certain of victory they'd worked until they dropped to bring it about.

There was talk of another German push and we all did what was called 'taking a grip on ourselves,' which meant simply being ready for anything and biting our nails as we wondered where it would come.

When it came however, the offensive was well to the south on the Chemin-des-Dames. It started on May 7th and in no time at all the French had lost everything they'd gained since October, 1914. Since we'd lost in April all the ground we'd gained after the slaughter on the Somme and a lot of the ground we'd gained from Passchendaele, spirits slumped again and it began to seem that the war wasn't so near ending as we'd thought. Down there the British were forced to retire to the Aisne and the French nearly to the Vesle, then suddenly the war woke up in our sector as well, as all hell broke loose to relieve the strain in the south.

The weather was poor, however, with cloud low and solid, and we'd all decided there wasn't a cat in hell's chance of flying a patrol when Wing rang up to find out what we were up to. Milne was orderly officer and was sitting by the telephone in the office reading a book, and he replied quite truthfully that we weren't doing anything very much.

'Just sitting around,' he said, and the man at Wing promptly insisted on speaking to the adjutant. When the adjutant arrived, he demanded to know why the squadron wasn't flying when all along the front men were dying.

'There's nothing we can do,' the adjutant said truthfully. 'We wouldn't be able to see a thing. The clouds are down to less than 1000 feet.'

'Aeroplanes can fly at 500 feet,' the man at Wing snapped, and insisted that a patrol should be flown at once – with bombs. 'It's the policy to harry the Germans,' he said.

It was Munro's turn for duty and he was furious because he'd already decided it was safe to go back to sleep, and he took off with his flight in a fury. The rest of us were at breakfast when they returned – soon afterwards because Munro had decided it was hopeless to try to fly a patrol.

'Damned armchair warriors,' he growled. 'It must be marrvellous tae sit back at base an' win medals an' high pay just by tellin' other bodies tae gae oot an' die.' He lit his pipe and tossed the match away. 'The war doesnae change much,' he added bitterly. 'We lost Walters.'

Walters was the youngster who'd walked away from his crash-landing after the scuffle with the Richthofen crowd, and he'd always had the look of a born victim. He was pale and good-looking with manners that had seemed too good for the rough and tumble of the war – not the gracious good manners of Ludo Sykes and his family, but the sort that sprang from being the only child of a doting mother, which in fact was what he was.

'What happened?' I asked.

'All we could do was drop the bangers and come back,' Munro growled. 'Ah just happened tae be lookin' round an' saw the kid do a sort o' roll an' spin intae the ground near the German line. Ground fire, Ah suppose.'

'No hope of him escaping?'

'No' a chance. I wouldnae ha'e crossed the blasted lines at all if I hadnae had the bombs.' Munro shuddered. 'Ah reckon Ah'll never get used tae death,' he ended.

At dinner that night we all politely disregarded the empty chair. No one mentioned Walters, and the conversation carefully avoided the war. But I knew just what Munro was feeling and just what Bull had meant when he'd quoted Donne. A man's death *always* diminished us, and though I always tried to pretend that by this time I'd grown calloused I knew I hadn't and it worried me.

–

I was in the lowest of spirits when a message arrived for me from the hospital at St Marion. It was from Charley to say she'd arrived and was there any hope of meeting? It seemed to me there might well be, and when it rained the next evening I drove over in the Major's car which he'd lent me for the occasion. Since we had a man there with a bullet through his calf it was a good excuse.

After I'd paid my respects to the wounded man and eaten more than I should have of a large fruit cake he'd had sent out from home, I made enquiries about Charley. The nurse was helpful and I was told to wait by the reception desk in the corridor outside the ward. She turned up within five minutes and I kissed her automatically.

She looked startled. 'What's that for?' she asked.

'Nothing,' I said. 'I always kiss you when I see you, don't I? It isn't the first time and I don't suppose I'm the only one.'

She gave me a long cool stare. 'As a matter of fact,' she said, 'you are.'

The words made me feel silly and a little like an overgrown schoolboy. I pretended to be unconcerned. 'Get your cape,' I said, 'and we'll go and have a meal.'

'You can only be joking.' She laughed but she sounded edgy. 'They only let us out in twos and then only in daylight. Nice young nurses aren't supposed to have boy friends, and as for having a date with one—'

'But we've known each other for ages,' I said.

'Makes no difference. If they found us going out with a male there'd be an uproar like the storming of the Bastille.'

'Your family never objected to me.'

'My family are in England.'

I was angry. Most of our time together had been spent in leg-pulling or acting the fool, but I'd been surprised to find just how delighted I was to see her because she'd seemed to bring a little colour and sanity into what was clearly becoming an extraordinarily stupid war run by people with ideas from the last century.

'If I can't take you out for a meal,' I snorted, 'I can't see much point in coming to see you.'

'My heart bleeds for you,' she said coolly. Then she went on in a quieter voice. 'Of course, you *could* go in for a bit of morale-boosting. When I arrived here I felt so damn' miserable I thought I could weep. It's all so cheerless and depressing and the wounded are so fresh from the battle. It makes it different.'

She looked at me with large eyes not far from tears and I realized how selfish I'd been. 'Gosh, Charley, I ought to have realized—!'

She managed a jagged laugh. 'You have your blind spots,' she agreed and I quietened down.

'What's it like?' I asked. 'From your end.'

She managed a rueful smile. 'Bit grim. Better than in England though, in spite. Everybody there seemed to be out of the top drawer or pretending to be, and determined to stay where it's safe. "Narse! Have you a minute to spah!" That sort of thing. Out here, at least everybody's trying. Acute surgical's the heaviest but acute medical's more wearing.' She frowned and it was almost like a wince. 'I wish some of those horrid old people back home who talk so glibly about honour and this being a holy war could just see the mustard gas cases.'

She made a brave effort to grin at me, but it didn't somehow work, and she stopped pretending. 'Everything seems to stink of iodoform and even after all this time I still don't enjoy seeing a man bleed to death before my eyes.' She blinked quickly as though tears were near the surface. 'I always open the windows when they've gone, Martin. To let their souls out. It's superstitious but I can't help it.'

She frowned again then smiled at me as though fighting to thrust it all behind her. She'd never claimed any intellectual pretensions but she was endowed with a great deal of humorous good sense and I knew exactly how she was thinking. In 1914 all our generation, both male and female, all of us disastrously innocent and pure of heart, had dedicated ourselves to the war because it had seemed a fine and lofty ideal to do so. But there had been over 600,000 casualties on the Somme and 500,000 at Passchendaele, and God alone knew how many others from Mons in 1914 to St Quentin in 1918, and thousands – millions more – in Italy, the Balkans, Mesopotamia, Salonika, Italy and in Russia and at sea. There had never been much future for us and we were as different as chalk from cheese from those people who were too old to fight and belonged to another era, and centuries older than those who were going to be too young to know the war. The patriotism that they talked so easily about at home was wearing a little thin with us by now, and while we had at first constantly made a conscious effort to rededicate ourselves after each awful disaster, now a lot of us didn't bother any more.

I looked up at Charley. She was staring at me unhappily. 'When's it all going to end, Martin? I never knew it was so big when I was in England. And I begin to get scared.'

'That they'll never let you out?'

'Don't be silly,' she said a little sharply. 'Our family's been fairly well walloped by this war, as you know. I doubt if we'll ever recover.'

'I know Ludo's mother had a whole mantelshelf full of photographs of people who'd been killed. His cousins and things.'

'Lulu's cousins,' she said tartly, 'were my brothers. Two of them. I adored them both. *You've* lost *your* brother.'

'And a few more,' I admitted.

'Suppose it happened to you?'

'It won't. *I'm* not going west.'

'That's the sort of rot you all talk,' she said sharply. 'It'll be the other chap. Never me! Is that what my brothers said? And your brother, and my cousins and all those others?'

She looked scared and seemed to need jerking out of the mood. 'Is there anywhere we can talk round here except in this damned public thorough-fare?' I asked.

'There's a room where we're allowed to meet boy friends. I doubt if there'd be even that but for the fact that some of us have brothers out here and the brothers began to kick up a fuss that they were never allowed to see their sisters.'

'Matron's fault?'

'Not really. She's as stiff as her starched hat but she's fair and kind to dummies like me. It's those awful hypocrites back home.'

I gave a hoot of laughter. 'You're beginning to sound like an old soldier,' I said. 'You'll soon begin to feel, like the rest of us, that this is home and England's a foreign country.'

The room they'd set aside was small but comfortable, but there were several other nurses there. Someone produced coffee and biscuits and Charley and I sat in a corner talking in low voices.

'What are you going to do when the war ends, Martin?' she asked.

'Dunno,' I said. 'Go on flying I expect.'

'How? They'll disband the Flying Corps and the navy and the army, and everybody'll be walking round looking for jobs.'

'They might keep *me* on.'

'Suppose they don't?'

'There's bound to be a lot of old aeroplanes lying about that nobody wants. Perhaps I'll buy one or two and set up a passenger service.'

'Where to?'

'France. Germany. Holland. Italy. You could fly there in two hops.'

'Who'd want to travel in an aeroplane?'

'I would, for one.'

'Would anyone else?'

'Why not? Aeroplanes are flying for hours at a time these days. Carrying bombs. Why shouldn't they carry passengers?'

She stared. 'I never thought of that,' she admitted.

'They've developed enormously in the last two years,' I pointed out. 'When I first flew they were like box kites – *old* box kites. If they go on at the rate they are doing, they'll be flying to America soon.'

She grinned and I realized we'd managed to put the war behind us. 'You're pulling my leg!'

'No, I'm not. Vimy bombers can carry a six-ton load at a hundred miles an hour for nearly twelve hours and I hear they've designed a new Handley-Page with four engines that can fly for seventeen. With extra tanks, buses like that could make it to the Azores, and probably even all the way to Newfoundland. Further still the other way with the wind behind 'em.'

She stared at me, caught by my enthusiasm. 'And you'd like to be among the first?'

I grinned. 'On second thoughts,' I said, 'the Atlantic's pretty big and I'm not much of a swimmer. Perhaps I'll stay in the service instead.'

'What's Ludo think?'

'Ludo seems to think they might find a use for a chap with my experience. Especially as I'm young enough for them to get full value before I peg out. That is, providing I don't get knocked off first.'

As she looked up at me, her eyes were serious and I even thought they were damp. 'Don't talk rot, Martin,' she said. As I rose to go she gave me a smile. 'It would be all right to meet you during the day sometime,' she said. 'So long as there was someone else with me. Could *you* bring someone else?'

I thought of Munro. 'Yes, I could. He looks a bit funny, mind. He has to walk with two sticks.'

'He sounds half-dead.'

'Don't you worry,' I said. 'Even with two stiff legs, Jock Munro's more alive than most people are with two bendy ones.'

—

Munro was delighted at the chance of meeting a girl. He had no family and was a lonely man but he was far from tongue-tied. Charley's friend was a girl from Bradford called Barbara Hatherley who had a marked northern accent, a bright cheerful face and a quick mind, and Munro was well on form so that the discussion over the meal became lively.

'In France,' Munro said, 'even fried eiggs an' chips has style wi' it. English girls ha'e never measured up tae yon sort o' thing. They havenae even lairned tae cook yet.'

'And look at Englishmen,' Barbara Hatherley retorted spiritedly. 'Standing in corners sucking their pipes and talking about dogs.' She turned to Charley. 'They haven't even found out yet how to make their houses draught-proof for us, have they, Sykes? What chance have girls in a man-made world?'

Charley laughed. 'Hatherley, what an ass you are!'

'You ought to be a suffragette,' I said. 'Votes for women.'

'*I would have been*,' Charley said. 'If I'd been older. If they don't give us the vote after the war I probably still will be.'

'Your chances are good,' Barbara Hatherley said. 'You see, when it's all over the men'll all come back like conquering heroes to take over where they left off, quite forgetting that we've been running the show while they've been away.'

'*I* shan't go back like that,' I said. 'I have no ill feelings about anything – except perhaps bully beef.'

'*You're* no' normal,' Munro pointed out witheringly. 'Y'always did think the world was full o' kind hearts an' sweet natures. What you need, laddie, is a steady girl.'

'He's got one,' Charley said at once. 'I'm her.'

Later as we walked back to the hospital she looked at me worriedly. 'You didn't mind me saying that, did you, Martin? I didn't mean it.'

I looked round, startled to find I was faintly disappointed. 'You *didn't*?'

'No. I just thought it might be a bit difficult for you, that's all. I thought you might have to start talkin' about that other girl – what was her name?'

'Marie-Ange?' I frowned. 'Charley, I find I can hardly remember her.'

'Does it worry you?'

'I feel it ought to.'

'Suppose she—?' She looked anxiously at me. 'Did you ask her to marry you or something, Martin?'

'Good Lord, no! It never entered my head.'

'It probably did hers,' she said dryly. 'There's nothin' so explosive as the emotional life of a girl – except perhaps a hand grenade. What would you do if she did?'

It seemed to need a little thinking about. 'She risked her life for Ludo and me,' I said slowly. 'That's all I know.'

–

Back at the field, as we were undressing by the light of the lamp, Munro sat on his bed and looked up at me. 'Nice girl, yon Hatherley,' he said. 'Sykes' cousin's a nice girl, too. You fond o' her?'

I thought I must be but I didn't know how much. 'I suppose so,' I said. 'She's a bit overpowering sometimes, mind – all that huntin', shootin' and fishin' stuff.'

He gave me a shrewd look. 'I shouldnae worry aboot that,' he said. 'That's just a façade, laddie. She's young an' she's no' sure of herself yet. If it were me, Ah wouldnae let her go. She's worth hangin' on tae.'

He was just about to blow out the candle when Bull appeared. 'Full squadron show tomorrow,' he said. 'With bombs. Pressure all along the line to relieve the troops in the south. We're trench-strafing, with the SEs up top to keep the Tripes off.'

The klaxon woke us all up while it was still dark, and the hut became a chaos of scrambling men, all searching for equipment and clothes and getting in each other's way.

'Must be something big,' Bull said.

'Dinnae sound sae damned enthusiastic,' Munro complained, staggering on his stiff legs to drag on a flying boot. 'It's a confounded nuisance havin' tae wage war at this time o' the morn.' He put his head out of the door and withdrew it with moisture on his hair. 'Ceilin' at nought feet,' he said cheerfully. 'They'll call it off.'

But they didn't, and the squadron took off in three flights, with half an hour between each. We climbed in and out of the cloud, and almost immediately Milne had to turn back with a spluttering engine. There seemed to be a lot of two-seaters out artillery-spotting but no Germans and we dropped our bombs on the German front line. Little flags of canvas began to flap in my wings as bullets came up from the ground, but there seemed to be no damage and we pressed on. In the distance was what looked like a swarm of bees which I knew to be a dog fight, but by the time we reached the spot it had dispersed, leaving a single column of smoke to stain the sky where someone had gone down in flames.

We climbed again towards Lille and passed a flight of SEs heading east looking for trouble, then over La Bassée we found a German two-seater, but it bolted into a cloud like a rat down a drain and we flew round and round like a lot of agitated terriers for a while, hoping for it to re-emerge. Growing bored with waiting, I spotted a group of Triplanes to the south and we climbed above them and, as we came down on them, I found myself on the tail of the leader. He banked steeply as I fired, gradually turned over on his back and dropped into a spin.

Munro's flight had been down some time when we got back and he was making out his report. He'd lost one man but a telephone call had come through from an artillery post to say he was safe but had wrecked his machine in landing.

Another squadron patrol followed in the afternoon and Bull shot down an ancient Pfalz.

'Send his name tae the VC department o' the *Daily Mail*,' Munro said. 'But dinnae tell 'em that the Germans are so runnin' oot o' aeroplanes all they could put up for him tae knock doon was one o' last year's numbers.'

The fact that the day had worked out well had done him good and when someone handed him a letter from Barbara Hatherley he began to play quietly on the piano.

> *'If you were the only girl in the world*
> *And I were the only boy——'*

It was one of the sickly-sweet songs that were in vogue, which almost broke your heart when you were a long way from home and probably wouldn't see the next day, the sort men bought records of when they went on leave to remind them of France and played over and over on the gramophone until wives or sisters or mothers broke them over their heads in desperation, unable to stand any longer the nostalgia they couldn't comprehend.

Bull threw a magazine at him. 'Give us something more cheerful,' he shouted. 'Not that lovesick ballad.'

Munro grinned and began to pound the piano again.

> *'Hans vos mein name und a pilot vos I,*
> *Oot mit Von Karl I vent for a fly.*
> *Pilots o' Kultur ve vos, dere's nae doubt,*
> *Each o' us flew in ein Albatros scout...'*

Delivered in a broad Scots accent, the mixture of dialects set everyone laughing.

> *'Ve looked f'r BEs for tae strafe mit oor guns*
> *Ven last I saw Karl I knew he vos dones*
> *For right on his tail were two little Sops*
> *Hush-a-bye-baby, on the tree-tops.'*

The party grew riotous but at dinner there was a sudden dampening of the spirits as the major arrived, accompanied by an army brigadier with a toothbrush moustache and eyeballs that looked as though they'd been boiled. There was no surprise when orders contained the information that a local push was to start the next morning and, as soon as the major had finished, the brigadier got to his feet to say his little piece.

'We've got to harry the Hun,' he announced. 'It's up to you chaps with your bombs...'

'Here we gae again,' Munro snorted softly. 'Same as last time – wi' knobs on.'

After dinner, the major called me into his office. The brigadier was there, jabbing his finger at a map and making the bold sweeps of an armchair warrior over the area of the lines. He nodded to me – not very enthusiastically because, I suppose, I was only small fry to a brigadier.

'This is where we're going forward,' he said. 'There's bound to be some opposition just here but your bombs will easily deal with that, of course.'

He seemed to be regarding the battle as if it were a football match and I saw red.

'There's no "of course" about it, sir,' I said angrily and he lifted his head and turned his boiled blue eyes on me.

'What's that? What's that?'

'For us this isn't just arrows on a map, sir,' I said furiously. 'At our level it's men and some of 'em won't be coming back.'

'Won't be coming back?' He stared at me as though I'd told him something that had never occurred to him before. 'You're sure of yourself, young man, aren't you?'

'Yes, sir, I'm sure.'

'Couldn't be inefficiency, could it, I suppose?'

It was quite clear there wasn't much point in arguing with him. 'No, sir, it couldn't. I've been doing this sort of thing a long time.'

He gave me a long hard stare and, changing the subject, stuck simply to what the plan was. He seemed less inclined to take anything for granted, though, after that, and when I went out, the major surreptitiously patted my back at the door.

'Well said, Brat,' he whispered.

We were awake until midnight occupied with target maps or working at the hangars with the fitters and riggers to make sure the machines were ready. Munro seemed gloomy as we climbed into bed. 'Ah think Ah've got the hump,' he said. 'Somethin's goin' tae happen tae me. Ah can feel it.'

We were briefed to bomb batteries and troops on the move and, despite low cloud next morning, we took off and flew east, following the contours of the land. I passed over horsemen and infantry waiting by white arrows laid out on the ground, then swept over the barbed wire system of the German line. The area over which we flew was a featureless landscape pockmarked with shellholes crowded so close together they ran into each other. They seemed to be still filled with water from the winter, and the litter and debris of four years of fighting lay everywhere – smashed guns, aeroplanes, broken wire entanglements and shattered vehicles. Ypres, recognizable by its star-shaped citadel was away in the distance and there didn't seem to be a single wall running north and south that had been left standing. Everywhere seemed to be as flat as a sheet with no houses, no trees, nothing.

Seeing men in grey uniforms, we broke formation to drop the bombs. The earth seemed to be enveloped already in smoke and leaping flashes of flame, and we were whirling about in the smoke only yards from each other as we tried to place the bombs and turn out of the blast to zoom away.

There wasn't much hope of finding the target in the confusion and I dropped my bombs where I could. Climbing, I just missed the roof of a collapsed farmhouse and zoomed above the reek to catch my breath. A column of grey-clad men were marching towards me and, joining another Camel whose squadron insignia I couldn't recognize, I swooped down on them, guns rattling. The column crumbled but fire came back from ditches and I saw splinters fly as I shot past in a wild rocking flight that was accompanied by lumps of wet mud from the explosions of the other Camel's bombs. The other pilot must have been caught by the blast, however, because I saw his machine cartwheel into the running Germans and burst into a scattering of burning wreckage.

Back at Puy everyone was artificially noisy because they were all still suffering from fright.

'Those ground gunners are getting better,' Milne said a little breathlessly.

'No, mon,' Munro pointed out. 'It's just that they've got a lot o' targets.'

The Camel I'd seen crash had obviously come from another squadron because everyone seemed to be back safe except for one man who'd had to force-land, and the machines that were undamaged took off again as soon as they'd been refuelled. The sky was still covered by unbroken cloud that kept us low and the fire from the ground was appalling. Since Cambrai the previous year when ground-strafing had first come into its own, the Germans had learned a lot of tricks, and with batteries and trenches for targets, machines were returning with the remains of telephone wires round their under-carriages.

'"Dear Mother, I am well",' Bull quoted grimly. '"But unless the staff let up a bit, I don't expect to be for long".'

'The trouble,' Milne said, 'is that you can't dodge.'

Milne was right. Casualties usually came from new pilots who hadn't acquired cunning, because at first you never saw what shot at you, and it took time to learn the trick. Aeroplanes had a habit of appearing and disappearing from nowhere, no matter how hard you watched, but in time you learned to see things, where to look, and what to do, and as you did so, your chances of surviving increased. With ground-strafing, however, skill and cunning acquired over months of service were no good at all because, as Milne said, you couldn't dodge and all too often it was the men with experience who were prepared to go in a little closer, who were hit.

We went out again in the glowing light of the early spring evening, the targets the same as before. I was more than glad to get rid of my bombs and climb up to where it was safe, but the German air force seemed to have wakened up at last and there were quite a lot of them about. Nearby, over Pilckem, an RE8 slogged past with a couple of Triplanes pecking away at it and, though I caught one and sent it into the ground in a shower of mud and scattered debris, even as the observer of the RE8 waved his thanks, his machine, more badly hit by the Tripes than he could have realized, began to break up. An aileron fluttered, came loose and dragged behind for a while before it fell away, then as it went the machine canted over on one wing and began a turn. Finally the wing itself began to crumble and I saw struts and wires come adrift, until finally it was only a tangle of wood and canvas twisting and turning towards the earth.

Feeling sick and swearing aloud in terror, I climbed out of the area but, as I did so, an explosion underneath my tail almost made me lose control. Somehow the blast had stripped the whole left side of the machine of its fabric and, as I lost height, the engine began to sound like a can full of stones. There was machine gun on a cartwheel just below and in front and, as I sank lower, I saw it swing round and the flashes as it fired. Holes appeared in the port wing and a flying wire snapped with a twang like a double bass. Kicking frantically at the rudder bar to put the machine-gunners off their aim, I swung towards the west, but as I did so oil began to spray in my face, blinding me as it smeared across my goggles. Snatching them away, I could feel the whole aeroplane grinding and shaking and, though the air-speed indicator was smashed, I knew I was fast losing flying speed.

The lines disappeared beneath me and, seeing a gap in the smoke, I headed for it. Fields appeared and finally, after what seemed a couple of lifetimes, I saw what looked like an aerodrome. It had FEs on it so I guessed it must be a forward landing field for the independent force. Not that it mattered to me.

I hadn't enough height to get in properly and when I tried to fly between the trees the damned aeroplane wouldn't do what I wanted and I hit them end-on. Down they went one after another like ninepins and there was a sound of splintering wood and twanging wires as the wings were ripped off to cling to the branches like a lot of dirty washing, then the fuselage, with me still inside it, bounced along the ground, the under-carriage gone, the tail unit flying behind like a flag on the end of a wire. What was left skidded into a ditch and, as the nose dropped, I banged my face violently on the cockpit surround and ended up hanging head-down inches from the stubble in the bottom of the ditch.

Two men in overalls who looked like air mechanics dragged me clear.

'You wounded, sir?' one of them asked.

'No,' his friend said. 'It's only his nose that's bleeding.'

My face black with oil, I staggered to my feet, lights going on and off in front of my eyes and quite certain I'd broken my neck and probably fractured my skull as well. Half-crying with rage, fright and self-pity, I noticed a car come to a stop nearby, then I found myself staring up at an enormously tall figure with a moustache. Vaguely I sensed it was familiar and important and then a vast voice boomed at me. I could hear it even over the sound of a Fee taking off.

'You all right, son?' it demanded.

I was still stumbling about, my eyes crossed, my knees giving way, unable to see properly for the wallop on my head, and the great rumbling voice seemed to rub a nerve raw.

'What the hell's it got to do with you?' I demanded hotly. 'And, anyway, since I've been flying out here ever since 1916, it's about time people stopped calling me "son".'

The officer said nothing and I was led away, still dizzy. The man who held my arm was laughing.

'What's so damn' funny?' I demanded.

'You,' he said. 'Telling *him* to go and boil his head.'

'Why?' I said. 'Who was it?'

'Only Trenchard. The man who built the air force. He was here on a flying visit. I expect you'll be court martialled and shot.'

The Fee squadron laid on a car and I saw the tall man they said was Trenchard telling the driver to go easy. He drove as though I were made of eggshells but I was still shaking when I got back to Puy. The mess was empty so I dug out the mess waiter and made him give me a brandy to steady myself. While I was sipping it, Munro came in, followed by a few others. He looked tired, depressed and angry, but he cheered up as he saw me.

'Y'all right, Brat?' he asked.

'Just,' I said.

'I was a wee bitty worried, forbye. I didnae want tae have tae ring yon hospital.'

'Look, Jock,' I said. 'If anything happens to me, go and see her, will you? Personally.'

He nodded. 'Aye, I'll do that. If ye'll do the same for me. Ah've never had o'er much time for gels, but yon Hatherley's a bonnie lass.'

Nobody was saying much and Munro lit his pipe with a scowl. 'Ah suppose ye havenae haird,' he said. 'But Bullo's gone.'

'Oh, no,' was all I could say.

'Hit from the ground. He went on fire. What was that thing he was always quotin'? "*Never send tae know for whom the bell tolls. It tolls for thee.*" He seemed to wince. 'It did, mon, too. Ah was thinkin' fine it was gaein' tae be me, and all the time it was auld Bullo.'

I don't know how he felt but if it was anything like me he was feeling like nothing on God's earth. He sat down at the piano and began to play and sing softly to himself.

'Oh, mother mair
Go mak' ma bed
Ma heart is sair wi' sorrow
Adoon the glen
Lie seven dead men
In dowry dens o' yarrow...'

Normally he only played popular tunes we could sing to or the roistering ditties that started after a mess party, and this was something new. His fingers

122

seemed sure for once, too, and hit the keys well, as though he was more moved than he could say.

'Bullo was a guid feller,' he said.

It was almost as though it were Bull's epitaph because then he stopped and stared at the piano for a moment, before lifting his hands and bringing them down on the keys with a crash.

'And when Ah tell them,' he began to sing.
'How wonderful y' are
They'll never believe me—'

In no time at all, as though they'd been waiting for it, there were two or three others round him, also singing, and as I left the mess they were roaring away.

'Take the cylinder out of my kidneys
The connecting rod out of my brain,
From the small of my back take the camshaft
And assemble the engine again.'

They were feeling better already. Bad as it had been, they were slowly recovering, and the songs were our way of equating death with life, the only way we had of bringing an accepted daily routine of hazard down to a ridiculous normality. They'd be all right again tomorrow.

Chapter 5

As it happened I didn't notice tomorrow when it came. I woke up in the night with a splitting headache and spots before the eyes and I couldn't even remember how I'd got that way. The next morning I was barely aware who I was and they decided I'd been severely concussed by the crash.

'After all,' the doctor said, 'it was pretty spectacular and it's going to cost the air force a fortune for those trees. You'd better stay in bed for a week.'

Since I had an excuse and had knocked down about forty poplars without killing myself they didn't shoot me for what I'd said to Trenchard. They didn't even court martial me. Trenchard always had a soft spot for his pilots, even though he drove them hard, and what I'd told him became a standing joke in the squadron and 'What the hell's it got to do with you?' became a sort of slogan around the aerodrome so that you could hear the fitters and riggers shouting it at the corporals whenever they were asked what job they were on. Munro made great capital of it and for a while I became known as the 'What's-It-Got-To-Do-With-You?' man.

The war seemed to have settled down and the German attacks seemed at last to have slowed. Still pushing ahead in the south, they had gobbled up an awful lot of land but suddenly it began to look as though they weren't going to capture Paris after all or break through and curl round to the coast, and everybody began to feel more certain that they really were exhausting themselves and that if we could only hold on the war could well end in 1919.

Things were looking so good in fact that the telegram that came for me was a shock. '*Father dying. Can you get leave? Mother*' was all it said and it shook me because for three years I'd been thinking all the time it was me who was going to die.

The major was sympathetic and, as leave had started again, he said I could have four days to get over the crash and attend to my father's business. I was dubious, feeling it was unfair to leave the fighting to everyone else, but Munro had no doubts at all about what I should do.

'Go, mon,' he said.

I'd decided to call on Charley to see if she had any messages to take home and Munro gave me an envelope for Barbara Hatherley. Rather unexpectedly he seemed to have got it rather badly and they were writing to each other every two or three days now and he was sneaking off to see her even when I wasn't going to see Charley.

'You beginning to fancy getting married?' I asked.

'Might be,' he admitted.

'Seems to be catching,' I said. 'Everybody's at it. Must be the war.'

He gave an embarrassed grin. 'Thought I'd better make my mark before I was killed in the rush,' he said. 'Mind, it's somethin' I never expected, but there y'are, the world doesnae stop turnin' just because there's a war on. Folk go on fallin' for each other just as if everything were normal.'

'And a damn' good thing, too,' I said.

'Ye'll mebbe give her my love and hand her this note,' he said, though I knew it was no note but a long epistle he'd laboured over for hours.

Charley was tired and in low spirits. The hospitals were full after the German offensives and the allied counter-attacks, and she'd been on her feet for hours at a time. 'There's such a flood of them,' she said despairingly, 'and only a handful of us, and just when we drop on our beds to fall asleep the air raids start and they come and chase us into the shelters. As far as I'm concerned, I'd willingly take my chance but they seem to think we have to be looked after like a lot of infants just because we're girls.'

She was full of the high hurt rage of youth and pink with anger, and I put my arm around her. 'Go on,' I encouraged. 'Cough it up. You can cry on my manly breast if you like.'

She smiled at last. 'That's a situation that doesn't arise very often,' she said more cheerfully. 'Perhaps I ought to exploit it to the full.' She drew a deep breath. 'Sorry for the emotional blood bath,' she went on, 'but we can't let the patients see we're tired or fed up and it's nice to let your good resolutions go whistlin' down the wind when there's a sympathetic ear around.' She stared at me and frowned. 'I'm just cross, I suppose,' she went on, 'because some damn' padre came along and had the gall to hold a service and submit po-faced dissertations on the fact that everyone still has to do their duty to God, King and Country.' Her eyes blazed. 'It'll be better for this world when that damned trio are quietly tucked away in a box and forgotten.' She gave a wry grin. 'I think I'm getting war weary but it's been so awful and I keep thinking of all those poor men in there.'

'Tell you what,' I said, trying to pull her leg as I always did in a sort of mock affection we'd always used and got used to. 'Think of me instead.'

She gave me a long cool stare. 'What makes you think I don't?' she asked. 'Because I do. All the damn' time.'

I was surprised by her intensity and tried to make everything all right again. 'Sorry,' I said. 'Never realized.'

She sniffed and managed an uneven laugh. 'Give my love to Norfolk,' she said. 'I wish I were comin' with you. Your old flame Jane's home, did you know? Ludo's got a new job and he's on leave, so you'll be able to see them all.'

'I'll give them your love, Charley,' I said, and then, without thinking about it, I kissed her properly – quite naturally and without any trace of embarrassment. Though I'd kissed her often enough before, there'd always been a faint feeling of dare-devilry about it as I'd thought what a dashing chap I was. This time it was natural and to comfort her because she was on edge, and it had the effect of calming her. She gave a big sigh and pushed me away.

'Oh, go on, you silly ass,' she said. 'If anyone saw us, they'd send me home in disgrace!'

'Court martial you,' I said.

She grinned. 'And shoot *you*.'

England seemed as foreign as ever. Though the old exhortation to 'Scrag The Hun' had given way to the more dogged 'Carry On, We'll Beat Them Yet,' there were still too many people around who hadn't been in the slightest affected by the war. The newspapers were still full of stupid letters from aggressive civilians and what the correspondents at the front didn't know they made up. None of them ever went far enough forward to learn what it was really like in the trenches, anyway, and their stories were all too often just sentimental rubbish about how the soldiers looked after their pets and how, though the barbaric Germans constantly fired deliberately at wayside crucifixes and often hit them, the figure of the suffering Christ was miraculously never touched. They were even still whining that the Germans didn't play fair – as if it were a cricket match and the Germans were using spiked balls. It made me think of what Munro was in the habit of saying.

'If it's a case o' playin' dairty or not survivin',' he always insisted, 'then Ah reckon we should hit him as quick as we can, as hard as we can, where it hurts most and when he isnae lookin'! An', if we get a chance, boil him in oil too, so that next time he'll keep clear of us. It might shorten the war.'

Even so, to read what was being written about the Germans was enough to make your blood boil, especially since the few prisoners I'd talked to had all seemed to be ordinary young men like me with no particular hatred in their hearts, except for their own staff, profiteers and politicians, a factor which seemed to be common to British, French, Italians, and everyone else who was actually doing the fighting.

In the train from London I remembered Charley. It was odd to think of her tired and low-spirited – lively, cheerful Charley, warm, happy, good-tempered Charley whom I'd always enjoyed seeing ever since the first day she'd made my hair stand on end with some unexpected and outrageous remark. She'd always made me feel I was interesting and important and had always greeted me with outflung arms and a yell of delight as though I were the one person she most wanted to see. Sykes had once asked me if she'd meant anything to me and I'd said no she hadn't. But she was changing so fast, dropping her youthful affectations one after another so quickly, I was no longer sure and I had to keep reminding myself that I was still only nineteen and not old enough to be thinking this way, anyway. And then reminding myself also that in the last four years I'd grown older than many men of thirty, and generations older than those who'd never seen anything of the war.

When I arrived at Fynling my father was being nursed night and day. He'd been overworking for some time and had had a stroke while doing army lecturing in Cambridge. They'd got him home with difficulty and it was clear he couldn't last long. I still found it hard to understand that it was he and not I who had succumbed to the war.

His face was wax-like and he was barely conscious but he was able to give me his instructions. 'Just in case, Martin,' he said. 'You know what a feather-brain your mother's always been with her painting.'

'I don't know what you're fussing about,' I said, suddenly aware that overnight I'd become the man of the family, the strong shoulder on which the other members leaned, and that now he needed me in the way that I'd needed him as a boy. It startled me and frightened me a little with the responsibility.

'You'll be up and about before long,' I said, but I knew he wouldn't and I spent the whole day paying calls on family solicitors and bank officials and talking in dusty, file-filled rooms about what my father wished done. My mother seemed lost. She'd always been so immersed in her work she'd never really been completely with us and she seemed bewildered now to think her prop was going. She looked older, too, and there was a lot of white in her hair which had started to come when my brother was killed, but she seemed to understand that I needed to get out of the house and was quick to point out, like Charley, that Jane was home.

I borrowed a bike and rode over, but even that fell oddly flat. Jane was there all right, prettier than I remembered her, with Sykes standing just behind her with his disarming smile, but while we all greeted each other with joy, it was tinged with a certain amount of sadness, too, because Jane's father had also been working too long and too hard without assistance and he'd been told he'd got to stop or he'd kill himself. He'd sold the farm and was already installed in the house in Littlehampton where we'd always gone for holidays, being looked after by Jane's elder sister, Edith, whose husband was now running a hospital in France.

'I'm just helping mother to clear things up,' Jane said, 'and then we'll join Edith while Ludo's in France.'

Sykes gave me a wry grin as she bustled off. 'What a clearing away there's been,' he said. 'Your father. Jane's father. If we survive this war, Brat, the world'll be ours for the taking. Have you decided what you're going to do?'

'Survive,' I said. 'That'll be enough for the time being. How about you?'

'I've got a new job. Frightfully hush-hush.'

'I meant after it's over.'

He paused, running his hand round the back of his neck where he'd been wounded in 1916.

'I don't know,' he said. 'There'll be Hathersett Hall to look after when it's all over because my father's no longer young, but I don't want to give up flying. Perhaps I can combine the two. I expect we'll finally have to sell the place, anyway, because by then the taxes'll be too high and people like me will be as out of date as the dodo.'

'Not on your life, Lulu,' I said.

'Out-moded aristocrats?' His eyebrows lifted. 'With the revolution in Russia? Probably all be guillotined, shouldn't wonder.'

He hadn't changed much, just quietened down a little, probably because he was a bit older and was married now.

'Still, you never know,' he went on thoughtfully. 'The British army's a strange institution and it always seems able to find a place for people like me. Perhaps I'll stay where I am.'

'I should,' I said. 'The air force needs you. Hathersett needs you. The whole world needs people like you.'

'My word,' he said mildly. 'You don't half flatter a chap.'

I grinned. 'You know what you always said: "The cavalry only exists to give a little tone to what would otherwise be a vulgar brawl." It's the same with the Sykeses. Like Charley, you brighten the day.'

He laughed again and touched the medal ribbons on my chest. 'You'll come out of this affair trailing clouds of glory,' he said. 'You're tougher morally and physically than all the rest of us put together, old son. And you were born for swirling capes and plumes and rattling scabbards and the clattering of hooves in the dark.'

'Good Lord,' I said, startled. 'Me?'

'Yes. You. So don't give it all up and go in for something as mundane as commerce. The air force's going to need a few tough-minded people like you around, old fruit, because when this lot's over all those stodgy old generals and admirals in the army and the navy are going to try to grab back everything they've lost to us and there's going to be a hell of a fight on when peace comes to keep the air force alive.'

'There is?'

'There is that!' He gave me one of his brilliant warming smiles. 'But, by the grace of God, in Trenchard the air force's got just the man to stop 'em.'

'Think he'll manage it?' I asked.

'I'll bet my boots on it. It'll be a hell of a fight, though. They don't like an up-and-coming young mob like ours telling 'em what they can do with their traditions, and they'll do all they can to tear everything down again, because there's a lot of political support in the House among the entrenched old guard.' Sykes grinned. 'Fortunately, Trenchard'll not let 'em get away with it, and a few people like you and me around to back him up wouldn't be a bad thing.'

'Not me,' I said. 'That's one thing that's for sure. He won't want me.'

Sykes grinned. 'I heard about that.'

'Who from?'

'The man himself. He laughed like a drain when he thought about it later. You made your mark there, old son.'

I began to see myself as a general already.

It was impossible to wait for my father to recover and equally impossible to wait for him to die. The doctor made it very clear to me that there wasn't much hope, but I had to go back. My father held my hand for a while without speaking, his eyes on my face as though trying to imprint it on his memory, and I sat like that until he fell asleep, then I tiptoed downstairs, picked up my bag, kissed my mother and left.

In London everybody seemed to know what was happening in France. 'There'll be another push,' a man told me in the buffet at Victoria station. 'And this time it'll take us to Berlin. You see. There'll be casualties, of course – a lot of 'em – but you've got to disregard those, like that damned crowd in parliament who're always shouting for a negotiated peace.'

'What are *you* shouting for?' I asked.

'Unconditional surrender,' he said firmly. 'Put the Kaiser in the Tower. We mustn't give up until then, no matter what it costs.'

'Are you likely to be called into the army?' I asked.

'Not me. I'm reserved.'

'I thought you might be,' I said.

With all the other old sweats humping their kit in stained ill-fitting uniforms, I went to join the leave train. I felt vaguely like a ghost, the ghost of Martin Falconer who'd joined up in 1915, still too young to vote but not too young to be killed, and I was only too glad to be away from all the background of hysterical flag-wagging and *Keep The Home Fires Burning* that was stirred up by people who were never in any danger of having to do anything else.

The war was making cynics of us all.

–

I arrived back in France at a bad time. The weather was growing warm and the days were bright with sunshine.

'And there are eighteen hours a day when ye can fly, mon,' Munro said. 'An' that means eighteen hours a day when we *do* fly. And just tae cheer y'up, laddie, the new Fokkers are beginning tae arrive.'

'What are they like?' I asked.

'No' a bit like they said.'

'They're not?'

'No. They're ten times worse. They're good, mon, and more than make up for the rotten pilots they've got these days. Ah reckon they're snatching back air superiority and there's no nonsense aboot mixin' it wi' 'em. You just get up as high as ye can, then dive intae 'em an' zoom away before they get ye. Mon, it's a gey fine feat if ye just stay alive. How was England?'

'Full of war workers all screaming for blood.'

'Oors or the Germans'?'

'I don't think they're fussy.'

'It sounds familiar.' He gestured. 'We've got a new chap in Bullo's place. Welshman. Know what he's called?'

'Jones?'

'How did ye guess? He's hot stuff. He's even smaller than me – about five foot nothin' in his stockinged feet – and has tae sit on a cushion.' He grinned. 'Ye'll have haird yon story aboot the chap who crashed a BE at Netheravon and when he had to write a report, put down that he got in the slipstream of a sparrow?'

I grinned, too. 'Yes.'

'This is him. David Lloyd Jones. They were so startled, he got away with it.'

Jones proved a lively little cricket of a man with black crinkly hair and bright opal eyes, and a scar down the right side of his face where it had been cut by flying glass when he'd flown through a Sussex greenhouse the previous year. 'There I was, boy,' he explained in his high lilting voice. 'With the cockpit full of broken chrysanthemums, fertilizer and glass. And the owner saying I had to pay for the blooms.'

He'd been a sergeant in 1916 when the Somme had decided him that he'd had enough, but he'd been in the army since 1913 and had joined the engineers as a drummer boy.

'Recruiting sergeant picked me up in the valleys, man,' he said. 'Weighed about twenty-two stone and wore a red sash and red, white and blue ribbons on his hat so that he looked like a prize-winning shire stallion at a county show. I thought, "There's feeding for you, Dai boy. If they build you up like that, it's time you joined." With me, though, it never took. I stayed small.'

Munro grinned. 'Ah think we can leave safely the squadron tae him the night,' he said. 'Ah'm away tae see Barbara. Fancy comin'?'

I'd just decided I might when I was handed a telegram. It was signed by an aunt of mine and it said '*Father died 10 am*'. I knew my mother would be sad that I hadn't been there but, after seeing so many men die in the last three years, I couldn't think that it mattered much. My father surely wouldn't have missed me. He'd been slipping into a coma when I'd left and almost the last thing he could have seen was his surviving son. Being there at the end wouldn't have made him any happier.

I arranged to send a telegram back, but I didn't feel like going out under the circumstances and in the end Munro went alone.

The next morning I got my fill of the new Fokkers.

—

Somebody had found a German headquarters at a farm called L'Enfer, near Wasquehal, and all three flights were to go across the lines and bomb it.

'It's well-named,' Milne said. '*Hell!* It'll be hell all right when we arrive.'

It wasn't as easy as it sounded, though. The place was marked and named on our maps because it wasn't in a village and, because Wing didn't want anyone to get wind of what was coming, we were to go over and back at a murderously low altitude.

'What about top cover?' I demanded, not liking the sound of it at all.

'There'll be two squadrons of SEs sitting above you,' the major said. 'Wing say they've fixed it. They'll be watching, and as soon as you go in they'll come down to cover you.'

I still didn't like the sound of it. L'Enfer farm was too deep behind the German lines for my taste.

'One dive,' I instructed. 'Then pull out and go for the lines like blazes. Rendezvous over St Rô.'

The bombs were put in the racks, held so that the vanes couldn't rotate. When they were released the vanes were whirled by the wind to detonate them. They weren't very big, though, and we stood watching the armourers, wondering if it would be worth it: me, my heart fluttering already, Munro, leaning on his sticks, his face as Scottish as a haggis with its plain features and gingery hair, Milne, pink and white and schoolboyish like Taylor, and Jones, small, round and eager as a terrier, the scar on his cheek livid with excitement.

'Let's make 'em jump,' I said impulsively. 'When I go down, keep with me and all release your bombs as close together as possible. Make a nice big bang.'

Jones' pale face, as Welsh as Munro's was Scottish, cracked in a grin. 'There's vicious for you,' he said. 'Think of the headache you'll give 'em, bach.'

'And no fooling about,' I said. 'Straight in and out. I don't hold with this Balaclava stuff Wing seems to fancy.'

We went across at a thousand feet, straight for St Rô, and I spotted the farm straight away. Glancing round I could see everyone in position except for one man who'd had to turn back with a faltering engine. I looked up but I couldn't see any sign of the SEs that had been promised and for a moment I was inclined to call the whole thing off. But if the SEs were there I knew what Wing would say if I did, and I decided in the end that there was no point in hanging about because someone would soon catch on to what we were contemplating and the telephones would start ringing on one or two neighbouring airfields. So I waggled my wings, waved and pointed downwards, and we went right down to five hundred feet and for the last mile followed the contours of the ground. I was holding my breath all the way but my bombs seemed to go straight down the chimney, and as I pulled away I saw others knocking the tiles flying as they went through the roof. Then the smoke and debris and dust burst through the windows as they went off one after another, and men began to run for the yard in terror, their arms round their heads, and a couple of horses stampeded down a lane.

As we lifted away, I glanced back. The place looked a mess with the roof off and the windows out, but what Wing hadn't told us was that they'd got anti-aircraft batteries all round the place and machine guns in every hedge-bottom and, although we'd surprised them out of their lives, they soon recovered and things started exploding everywhere. Something went off under my tail and I thought I was going in, but I managed to drag the machine upwards with strips of canvas flapping, and spotting a hole in the clouds, went through it like a ferret into a rabbit hole. Munro knew me well enough to stay with me and Jones wasn't slow either. He was a little behind but he stuck close, and, as I turned and counted noses, I saw to my amazement that we'd all got clear away.

I was just congratulating myself when the man on my right came up alongside and waggled his wings and pointed, and I felt my heart go cold because just up above I could see a good dozen and a half German aeroplanes coming down on us. They had aileron extensions which made them Fokkers, an extra lifting space between the wheels, and long centre section struts like Vs that went to the base of the fuselage. They were the new DVIIs and as my eyes flickered round, looking for that top cover Wing were supposed to have laid on, I realized that some dim-brained idiot had once more made a hash of it and forgotten.

As they smashed into us, the whole lot of us split up and I could hear the appalling pop-pop-pop of machine guns as I zigzagged away. My Aldis was shattered and there were gaping holes in my left hand bottom plane, but I seemed to have come out of it alive. Then I heard another crack-crack-crack behind me in a higher note, as though it came from a different position, and splinters from a centre section strut flew into my face. A landing wire broke and the ends clattered and something tore the sleeve of my coat.

By this time I couldn't tell whether the bullets were coming down from the Fokkers or up from the ground. Then the engine spluttered and I switched to gravity, functioning automatically but still with a feeling that I was going to be dead very shortly. There were bullet holes everywhere now – one group close to the wing root – and a strong smell of petrol, but then the engine picked up again and I decided that perhaps I was safe after all. I could still hear the cracking noise behind, though, and looked round in a panic to see who was shooting at me. But I could see no one and was wondering if the machine was falling apart, and had just throttled back for safety when I realized it was a strip of torn fabric flapping on the fuselage just behind my head. The wing seemed to be coming loose by this time and I was just preparing to crash-land when, instead, I decided to chance it and opened the throttle to climb away. There was still a smell of petrol, however, so as we drew clear I cut the power again and crept along cautiously, and gradually even the racket behind me subsided.

Milne appeared alongside, then another man. I waved and another man appeared and yet another and I realized I'd still got everybody with me. I looked around. Just above, to the right another complete flight was forming up, and on my left, well behind but unmolested, there was yet another – less the one man who'd had to turn back at the beginning. We seemed to have escaped without casualties.

I was glad to reach Puy, terrified all the way the wing might collapse. In fact, as I touched down, it dropped and I thought it had fallen off at last, but instead it was the whole aeroplane that had tilted. As I switched off, the machine swung round in a ground loop and came to a standstill, and as I jumped out I saw it was because one of the tyres had been punctured, too.

The other machines were coming in past me now, rocking their wings as they taxied to the hangar. They all seemed to be safely back and, after a while, a Crossley tender began to bounce across the grass. Munro and Milne climbed out of it.

'Y'all right, mon?' Munro asked.

'I think so,' I said, still quivering like a jelly.

'Landin' like that's getting tae be a habit forbye. Ah hope ye say y'r prayers at night.'

'Not half.' I managed a shaky grin. 'God's a good friend of mine. He lets me down now and again but I suppose even He's not infallible. How about everybody else?'

'All down,' Milne said. 'All safe! But there's going to be a lot of hard work in the hangars tonight and tomorrow. The major's playing hell on the telephone to Wing about that top cover that didn't turn up and he's taken us off the roster for tomorrow to repair the damage.'

'An' me,' Munro said firmly, 'Ah'm gaein' intae St Marion tae see Barbara.'

I looked round. I was still shaking and had to fight to control it so that they wouldn't see it. There was a scorched tear down the sleeve of my coat, a piece out of the centre section strut inches from my face, several cut bracing wires, the group of holes near the wing root, the petrol tank holed near the top, two holes in the floor of the cockpit and about forty-odd others distributed about the aeroplane.

'What's yours like?' I said.

'Aboot the same. So's everybody else's.'

I drew a deep breath and began to laugh — a little too loudly to be natural. 'I think we must be the luckiest beggars in France to get away with that lot,' I said. 'I see what you mean about the Fokkers.' Clutching Munro, I did a wild dance of relief. 'And just hang on, old son, because I'm coming with you!'

–

Even as the German offensives waned and they were stopped dead by the Americans on the Chemin-des-Dames at Château Thierry, the war in the air seemed to step up. The weather grew warmer and the birds sang as the poppies flared among the clover and, with the Germans throwing all their resources into producing the deadly new Fokkers, an unexpected viciousness began to enter the fighting as the German pilots lashed out with an air of desperation.

Suddenly there was a gleeful note in the newspapers as they described how the blockade was growing tighter and the Germans were being forced to spread candle grease on their bread instead of butter. But with Russia out of the war, there were also vast numbers of troops who'd been freed from the east to hold us back in the west and it was obvious there was still a lot of suffering ahead – which was something the newspapermen never thought fit to mention.

There seemed to be little peace anywhere these days, in fact, because over the ominous tap of machine guns, the roaring of the guns to the east went on all the time, the sound filling the sky, the glare of their flashes tinting the clouds at night, so that the heavens seemed permanently red with flames. The bombers were overhead every night, too, either British heading for Germany or German trying to find the ammunition dumps. One night they found one at Vaervicq and we were all outside the mess watching the fireworks when the major called me to his office.

'You've done some night-flying, haven't you?' he said.

'Yes, sir. Over London with BE12s. When the Zeppelin scare was on.'

'Well, they've organized a specialist squadron near Abbeville and they've asked for you.'

My jaw dropped. 'But I've only just got back here!'

He shrugged. 'Special request. Nothing I can do. I gather it's only temporary. They want a few experts until they can train the newcomers. You're to report at once.'

Munro was furiously indignant. 'That's the damn' service all over!' he stormed. 'Just when I was beginnin' tae feel ye were a sort of good luck charrm, too!' Wondering what was ahead, I packed my kit and the tender dropped me at the new field late the following day. The major was a man called Brand but there was a lieutenant-colonel organizing things in the background, it seemed, and I was told to report to him. A strong suspicion was already forming in my mind and it was no surprise when I saw who it was.

'Lulu!'

Sykes grinned. 'Asked for you particularly, old boy,' he said. 'Germans have become quite bad-tempered with their heavy bombers just lately and I've been sent out to organize the opposition. Thought you might help. I've organized a night fighter unit—'

'What the hell are night fighters?'

'Same as day fighters. Camels with knobs on. And why not? After all, we did quite well with those fearful BEs. Why can't we do better with Camels?'

'How do we get up and down?' I said. 'I seem to remember that was always a problem.'

'Special lights. Better flare paths. Try it and see. Ought to be rather jolly.'

It was a bit nerve-wracking at first, getting a machine as unstable as a Camel off the ground in the dark, but Sykes had at least given us more than a piece of string tied to the centre section for instruments and, with special phosphorescent dials, it was possible now to tell which way up we were flying. He'd also taken the Vickers guns off the cowling where the muzzle flash would dazzle us in the dark and mounted two Lewises on the top wing in their place. Getting down was easier, too, because he'd organized decent flares and a proper system so there was no danger of hitting each other in the dark. I even began to feel optimistic.

There were a few alarms and we went up a few times but we always seemed to be in the wrong place at the wrong time and we never saw anything.

'If only we could get these radio chaps to tune in on 'em somehow and tell us where to find them,' I said.

Sykes stared at me. 'How?'

'I dunno how,' I said. 'Some sort of signal that would play a note on their flying wires or their engines or something, and come back so we could pick it up. Or a noise detector. The army have listening posts to pick up enemy telephone messages. Something like that so we could follow 'em round in the dark.'

He grinned. 'Come back in the next war,' he said, 'we'll see what we can do.'

I shrugged. 'No, thanks,' I said. 'That one'll be a lot different, and I hope I'm not in it because it'll be dangerous. They'll have real aircraft then – aircraft where you can leave the wheels behind or something when you take off, so you've no drag.' I grinned. 'Lulu, that's a hell of an idea – no wheels hanging down – think of the increased speed.'

'You always did have ideas ahead of your station, Brat,' he smiled. 'Let's concentrate on what we've got.'

We continued to wait, chasing about in the dark, perfecting the technique and training newcomers. There were a few accidents, mostly coming down, but nothing serious because Sykes had thought a great deal about it and everything was well organized. Then suddenly, just when things were going well, he was taken off the job.

'Middle East,' he said with a rueful grin. 'They've got something they need clearing up there. Fearfully exciting. Fancy coming with me?'

'Not really,' I said. 'I think my job's in France. And flying day fighters, too, come to think of it. I'm wasting my time here. I can do more damage where I was.'

He laughed. 'Good old Brat,' he said. 'Unparalleled ferocity as usual. Give my love to Charlotte.'

And then he was gone, leaving everyone feeling bereft as usual, because of his charm, and me with a determination to get back to my own squadron.

Since the thing was organized and working well now, Brand said I could go at the end of the week and I began to pack my kit again. But that night the bombers were over again and, as they found the ammunition dump at Marigny and started to plaster it, we all started running for our machines. The whole sky seemed to be going up in flares of white and red and yellow, and the earth under my pounding feet felt as though an earthquake was taking place.

We got off the ground in a hurry, going up like lifts, the Camel vibrating madly under the strain as I forced every inch of climb out of her. I soon lost the rest of the squadron who were heading west, even the man I was supposed to be working with, a captain like myself called Yuille, but I was able to use the fires burning on the ground for a horizon, and sitting up there in the darkness, with the wires and the leading edges of the wings faintly picking up the light, I reflected that we still had a long way to go before night fighting was going to be much good.

Finding my height, I flew east, deciding that the Germans must swing round and head homewards after dropping their bombs, so that I would be across their path; and sure enough, half an hour later, half-frozen and beginning to grow bored with the darkness, I saw a huge aeroplane just emerging from the scattered clouds towards Abbeville, an enormous machine big enough to take my breath away, like a vast dark cross just above me, with a wing span that seemed to fill the sky.

At first I thought it was one of the Gothas which I knew well from the raids on London, but then I saw it had five engines, one in the nose and two each in nacelles between the huge wings. Uncertain what it was, I made a wary turn, looking for the guns. It seemed to have firing positions in the nose, in the fuselage and on the top wing, and I guessed the wingspread to be around a hundred and fifty feet. It also had a biplane tail and a nose wheel, which was something I'd never seen before.

Opening the throttle, I began to climb towards it. Our combined speeds must have been in the region of two hundred miles an hour and there was no time to manoeuvre for position, so as soon as I came up close I pressed the button. As the guns jumped and rattled and I smelled the cordite, I knew I'd hit it but I also knew that it was so big it would need a lot of bullets to do any damage, and I found myself longing again for something that would fire small explosive shells to blow chunks off it.

The huge aeroplane was turning slightly now, away from me, and as I came in again a searchlight sprang up, blinding me with the overspill. Then another and another and another. I swung away, afraid of colliding, and when I looked again they were holding the German like a huge white crucifix in a cone of light just above me.

'I bet that makes them blink a bit,' I thought.

I was over Abbeville now and I wondered where the other fighters were because my petrol was running low and it would soon be time for me to land. But, just then, I saw another machine astern of the German, coming in fast, and I decided that if I could have just one more go close in, it would keep the gunners busy till he arrived.

As I went in, they saw me clearly in the light and there seemed to be so many bullets flying around I couldn't make out why they didn't hit me. There were at least six guns firing at me and as little flags of fabric began to flutter on the wings I decided it was safer to get out again and flipped the Camel over in a tight turn with the wings flat against the sky.

As I did so, I caught a glimpse of the other fighter close behind the giant's tail, in the killing position, and even as I looked he must have fired because I saw a sudden flare of flame start in one of the German's wing nacelles, quite distinct as a bright glow against the sky.

As I caught my breath, the big machine tilted over on one wing, lumbering and slow, as though manoeuvring were difficult because of its size, then it went into a shallow dive towards the east. Still watching, I saw its slow turn grow steeper and the nose drop abruptly. Pieces broke off – first one or two and then more and more – and, yelling excitedly above the roar of the engine, I saw them fluttering down in the flare of the searchlights. One of the huge wings began to crumple – at first merely sagging, then concertinaing as though it were tired – and the machine was carried round the debris by the remaining good wing so that the aeroplane was doing a flat spin. Then the good wing crumpled, too, and the huge nose dropped and the vast machine went down like a huge flaming torch, growing smaller and smaller in the darkness until

I saw it thump into the ground near Abbeville and the glow of flame as it exploded.

Yuille was already down when I got back and he grinned as I appeared. 'My God, man,' he said, 'you didn't have to go in *that* close! I thought you were trying to shoot him down with your revolver!'

There was no doubting the victory and Yuille was given due credit for it, and the party that started went on into the early hours of the morning. The following day we learned that the machine was a Staaken, one of the giants built by the Zeppelin works when their airships had proved such a costly failure. Someone had gathered some data and we seemed to have done a real giant killer act. There had only been a few built and it had five Maybach engines and carried a ton of bombs, with a wingspan of a hundred and eighty-three feet and a length of seventy-four. It had six machine guns, as I'd decided, a crew of five and carried parachutes – two of which had actually been found – fastened to fixed positions with static lines, so that they operated like those in observation balloons.

'My God,' Yuille breathed enviously. 'Parachutes too! What's the war coming to?'

'Perhaps the Germans aren't so damn' silly as our side to send pilots up without 'em,' I said.

'They might even give 'em to fighter pilots before long,' he grinned. 'There are a few chaps at the top now who've actually flown in action and they know damn' well that a parachute – even a poor one that's none too reliable – is better than nothing at all.'

One or two pilots went to see the wreckage but I decided that, with the flames and the speed with which the Staaken had hit the ground, there wouldn't be anything left to look at, and also, by this stage of the war, smashed aeroplanes only served to make me think it might be my turn next.

Because of the success, a man from Wing came to try to persuade me to stay with the squadron but I didn't like night fighters and, fortunately, at that moment the war woke up again and someone at headquarters decided I'd better go back to where I was most use.

Munro fell on me as if I were a long-lost son, but the party he planned to celebrate the return of the prodigal came to nothing because the same day the army took a marked aversion to observation balloons and demanded that they be knocked down all along the front. Knowing what was ahead of us we went quietly to bed instead. Balloon strafing was never a popular job because the ground around them was always crammed with anti-aircraft and machine guns, and on the first of the forays Taylor was wounded and on the second one of Munro's flight was seen to dive into the ground.

Munro's anger took the form of a baffled glare. 'Ah reckon the war'll only end when we run oot o' men,' he said. 'When the last two fellers are standin' up in the ruins sloggin' at each ither wi' clubs like stone age warriors because we've run oot o' guns.'

The next day Richthofen's lot turned up again.

–

The morning was cool and overcast with a strong west wind pushing a blanket of misty cloud before it, and the front line was marked with the grey wool of smoke from exploding shells streaming before the wind so that as I led the squadron north it was difficult to tell exactly where the line lay. Then I saw swarms of khaki-clad figures edging forward in little groups, clotting at the wire, or behind ridges and ruined buildings. Behind the German lines troops were moving up with columns of carts and gun limbers. Near Wervey we caught a battery of guns in a sunken road, and as we swung back over them to study the damage, my stomach turned as I saw the tangle of harness and guns and the struggling, screaming, dying horses.

The evening patrol was a high one for a change, with Munro and Jones tagging on behind. Seeing a large formation of brightly-coloured Fokkers south of Lille, I went for them and for once they didn't disappear eastwards. As we dived I saw a Camel spin away, then a red Fokker with brown wing tips slid sideways in front of me, like a duck rising out of the weeds. As I fired automatically, it flopped on its back and hurtled downwards like a square-winged coffin.

For a while the sky was full of aeroplanes in a whirling hubbub of machines. Diving Fokkers, all the colours of the rainbow, drifted across in front as I kicked at the rudder and pressed the trigger, then as the fight broke up a flight of SEs arrived, going through the scattering aeroplanes, guns clamouring, and we were alone again with the Germans dropping out of the sky towards the east.

We made our way back to Puy in twos and threes and it was hard to tell who was missing and who was not. My own flight came back unscathed except for a few holes, but after the sudden descent from the height we'd been at, we all felt faint and exhausted and when the blood got moving properly in our veins the feeling was agony. Jones had lost a man and Munro had lost Milne. I was sorry to hear it because Milne was showing signs of becoming quite good, with every chance of surviving the awful period of a newcomer's initiation.

'Makes y' understand why we get flying pay,' Munro said slowly. 'Naebody wi' any brains would do what we do f'r less. It's like goin' o'er the top three times a day.'

'What happened to him?' I asked.

'Hit the ground somewhere near Meulebeke.'

'Could he have got out?'

He shook his head in a dour dogged way, then he sniffed and lit his pipe, low in spirits suddenly.

'They have *their* teams o' killers,' he went on slowly, 'and *we* have oors, and we all ken weel that whate'er happens some puir wee body's gaein' tae get hurt. It reminds ye o' those gladiator laddies the Romans used tae have. All professionalism, technical skill, expertise, cold-bloodedness, indifference an'—' he sighed '—an' a weariness of killing.'

Chapter 6

The next day it started all over again. The Germans were persisting with their offensives but it seemed now that their attacks were being made with a feeling of desperation. Down in the south they'd been stopped dead, and on the Italian front they were actually being pushed back so that it seemed that any further offensives they undertook could be nothing but a gamble.

As the weather grew hotter, they attacked between Paris and the Meuse but their offensive was smashed and the allies began to counter-attack and then, to everybody's surprise – because, although we'd been expecting something of the sort for a long time, we'd never dared to hope it would come off – the whole front came to life in a counter-offensive and for the first time we saw the Germans not merely retreating but actually reeling back in confusion.

'It's happenin', mon!' Munro said in an awed voice. 'It's happenin'! Ah never thought Ah'd live tae see the day! Ah honestly think it's comin' tae an end.'

That night the place went mad. Despite the few older men who were appearing now, the squadron – like most of the squadrons along the front – by the very nature of the game was still composed of boys barely out of their 'teens. From the pinnacle of old age where three years of front line flying had placed me I sometimes felt, forgetting how young I was myself, that their hotheaded youth was heart-breaking, but it also had the advantage that there were always willing helpers when someone wanted to organize a party. That night Jones proved to be a rival to Munro as a musician. Having joined the army as a drummer, he'd also learned to play a few other instruments and he could raise the roof with the trumpet. His nose pushed out of joint a little, Munro challenged him to play *God Save The King* standing on one leg, and he not only stood on one leg but he did it on a stool balanced on a chair, playing the trumpet with one hand and balancing a billiard cue on the tip of the first finger of the other.

All might still have been well but Munro grew ambitious, and, not content with thumping on a piano, he acquired a set of bagpipes from somewhere and the sound of the two of them standing on the table trying to play *Land of Hope and Glory* was enough to bring in the pilots from the Bristol squadron to start a battle with flying pieces of bread. 'Och, the fine sound,' Munro was saying proudly as the table collapsed.

Jones was as mad as a pilot as he was as a musician and it was his pleasure to chase hares across the fields at an altitude of nought feet, in the same way that he liked to chase staff cars down the roads. It was a daring that came from over-stretched nerves – because he'd been out since February – and it was the sort of manifestation of thinly-disguised fear that worried me, because I'd always believed that aeroplanes, like motor cars, were lethal unless properly used – even to the people who were controlling them.

'There's kind of you to warn me,' he smiled when I said I thought he ought to cut it out. 'But we all know there are no Welshmen in heaven, boyo, and Dai Bach isn't expecting to die with his boots off. I'll chance it.'

There was plenty of opportunity because the allied generals suddenly seemed to be scenting victory and they began to throw everything they had at the Germans and, with the brilliant weather, there were no periods of calm when we could recover a little. Before, it had always been possible to think about what you were going to do, make plans about how best to tackle a job and decide on methods of attack. But not now. Now it was just a dogged grinding slog to drive the Germans out of the sky and out of every fortification they tried to build and hold. Previously, men with bright ideas had been listened to, and I'd come up with a few myself, but now we simply went headlong into everything, accepting casualties so that the Germans should not be allowed to recover and make a stand. There was no room for intelligence, just bull-headed attacks, and there wasn't even time to think much, because 'shows' were called for again and again, sometimes two or three a day.

Machines began to falter and nerves grew ragged, and men were killed as judgement failed. There was an appalling accident right in front of our eyes when one of the Bristols just coming back from the line after destroying a Fokker, started to shoot the place up as a gesture of triumph and broke up right over the aerodrome. The wings snapped back and it dipped forward abruptly so that the crew were jerked out. I thought they were going to drop on me and started to run, but they hit the ground just behind and I could hear the heavy double thud for the rest of the night.

The list grew all the time. Even the men who came from England told of crashes in which someone whose name was known had been killed. The whole war in France had taken place for four years in a narrow strip of churned-up land three hundred miles long by ten miles wide so that the old hands all seemed to know each other and everyone who fell out of the sky or killed himself in some stupid accident caused by tiredness and relaxed alertness was just another jab at the heart. Every time we entered the mess, someone seemed to say 'Remember old so-and-so? Flew into a hangar at Hendon while he was taking off,' or 'Remember George Whatsisname? Student pilot landed on top of him while he was taxiing at Shoreham.'

The staff were still pushing for absolute command in the air. At long last someone had realized that the air force had a part in the scheme of things and that, without command up above, no one would ever have command down below, and the long hours of daylight and perfect weather with no days off brought increased casualties, so that Munro looked worriedly at me more often, as I did at him, and we both began to wonder if we'd outlived our luck. Over to the east the whole countryside seemed to be falling apart under the bombardment and still the staff demanded more, and more, and more.

It was August now and at last the French had regained Soissons and were still moving forward. But, though you had to go twenty miles behind the German lines to find anything, Wing still insisted on us going to look.

Munro was baffled. 'What yon Germans think they're defendin' there Ah cannae imagine,' he said. 'But ye can always trust yon oily beggars o' the staff tae send us after 'em.'

He was looking exhausted now, his face pale and his eyes sore with too much flying. And at night he was muttering in his sleep so that he woke Jones and me. When we stirred him out of his nightmares, he looked at us shamefacedly. 'Ah keep dreamin' Ah'm on fire,' he said.

He could still bang on the piano, though, and get the sing-songs going, which was as much as anyone wanted these days. None of us had the energy to leave the aerodrome and indignant letters came to me from Charley demanding to know what she'd done and why I hadn't been to see her. She'd done nothing; in fact she was the one person I wanted to see just then more than anyone else, but I couldn't drag myself off my bed or out of an armchair once I'd fallen into it. Energy seemed to have gone and her cries grew more indignant, so that I'd just decided I'd better do something about it when orders arrived for us to leave Puy and move east out of reach to a new field at L'Escoril.

With the advance going well, we weren't allowed to waste the good weather just in moving house and we flew a patrol on the way. The new field was empty and comfortless and we settled into our new quarters aware of the absence of the familiar things we'd had to leave behind which, though they'd never been luxury, at least had made the place feel like home.

I was sleeping badly myself by this time but Munro was having the most awful nightmares now and kept jumping out of bed, sometimes half-a-dozen times a night. Taffy Jones and I kept stuffing him back and he kept apologizing until the hut was full of self-deprecation.

'I cannae help it,' he kept saying miserably. 'I keep dreamin' I'm on fire so I jump.'

'We could always tie you in by yere, boy,' Jones suggested, indicating the bed spring.

'Oh, aye,' Munro said. 'That'd be marvellous. I'd break ma neck just fine.'

'No, no! Just loosely, you understand, so you'd feel the tug of the string as you tried to get out and wake yourself up.'

Munro gave a twisted grin. 'That's it!' he said. 'Taffy, mon, ye've got it!'

That night he secured himself to the bed spring with the cord of his pyjamas. It didn't help much, however, because as he jumped out it dragged his trousers down his legs and held his feet fast so that he came down with a thump on the floor on his chin and knocked himself unconscious.

Jones stared down at him from his own bed. 'There's daft for you, boy,' he said mildly.

We picked him up gently and stuffed him back again. 'How about asking the Doc for a sleeping draught or something?' I suggested.

'A sleeping draught!' Munro was just coming round and he was indignant. 'There's only one sleepin' draught tae a Scot, mon, and yon's a large Scotch whisky.'

He was putting on a good show of indifference but his nerves were clearly in rags. Three tours in France was a lot, because every time you grew tired more quickly than the last.

Then news came that Mannock had been killed. 'Flew into the ground while ground-strafing,' Munro said. Then, of all people, McCudden, one of the safest men in the business, who, it seemed, had lost his engine on take-off. They'd both become legends in their own time, like Ball and Bishop and Richthofen and Voss and Guynemer, and the realization that men of such ability could be killed shook the confidence out of us again. I'd known McCudden personally. He'd been around since the first days of the war when he'd gone to France as a mechanic, and he'd risen step by difficult step through the ranks to major through sheer courage and ability. He was probably one of the greatest of all, cool-headed, calculating, a regular who picked his victims and never took risks. Mannock was just the opposite, never an individualist, but a born leader who inspired his men and hated the Germans with a genuine loathing.

That night Munro had another of his nightmares.

'Ah reckon Ah'm dyin' o' funk,' he said.

But it wasn't funk. It was flu. It was spreading all over Europe suddenly and was supposed to be killing the half-starved people in Germany in thousands. It was also rife among the troops, the worst hit always the oldest soldiers, the ones who were most likely to be exhausted and least able to resist.

Munro seemed thankful it wasn't anything worse. 'Ah thought mebbe it was mange,' he said.

'Shouldn't let it worry you,' the doctor said cheerfully. 'Half the army'll be down with it before long. Pyrexia of unknown origin, some people call it. Personally I think it's just plain damn' war weariness.'

We spent the whole night watching Munro alternately shaking as though with ague and sweating violently in a temperature. By the next day six other men had gone down with it, too, and

174

what with the disease and the sheer weariness of the ones who were left, the mess was pretty quiet for a long time because there were only enough of us left to work two flights on alternate patrols.

'There's cunning for you, man,' Jones said, shaking his head solemnly over Munro. 'Earmarking the worst time of the war to be ill.'

'Look you, inteet to gootness, ye silly Welsh fatheid,' Munro hooted. 'Ah didnae earmark it, it earmarked me! How's the war goin' anyway?'

'We're due for another move forward any minute,' I said. 'Before long we'll be taking over old German fields.'

'I hope they leave us some Rhine wine, boy,' Jones said.

'They say it's the beginning of the general offensive to win the war,' I pointed out.

'This year?' Munro asked.

'Next.'

'How aboot the flyin'?'

'Mostly at sparrow altitudes.'

'It's daft that staff is,' Jones snorted. 'I don't like flying through wet grass, boyo, and there are so many aeroplanes about these days, bach, it's like

Piccadilly Circus. You can almost spit in their eyes as they go past. I nearly did today.'

'Who was it?'

'I don't know. They come and go so fast you don't get time to know 'em. We've lost Smyth and Duckworth and that new youngster – what was his name now? – and that feller who stayed so short a time, indeed I never did learn what he was called.'

Munro managed a weak grin. 'So long as *you* don't go, Taffy,' he said. 'You and Brat here.'

It was true we rarely flew much higher than two thousand feet these days, tearing along in a new kind of war down the roads, fired at by machine guns, and smashing through the ground fire to shoot and bomb anything that moved. I was finding it all very wearing and wishing even that I could have a comfortable dose of flu and retire to bed.

To add to the work, the major also went down and, being senior flight commander, I had to take the squadron over until he recovered. Twice I'd run a squadron for short periods, but this time the trivia of reports, returns, records and the problems of repairs, the worries of the NCOs and armourers, fitters and riggers, and the shock of casualties and the problem of replacements who knew so little about flying they couldn't possibly have been sent over the lines without practice all seemed worse than before. It was because I was growing tired. I'd never thought I could grow tired like this. I'd been weary at the end of my first stint in France but this time the worries seemed insurmountable and the work was a dead weight round my neck.

I hardly seemed to have time to breathe and one evening when I'd got through the office routine early and was heading for the mess, Munro, who was just beginning to make his shaky way about the field, caught me by the arm and led me off to the hangars with some query about spares he could quite easily have handled himself. I decided in a fury that the flu had gone to his head and, leaving him cold to deal with it, headed back to the mess. This time it was Jones.

'Transport,' he said.

'What about transport?'

'It's got to be settled,' he said, and delivered a lengthy dissertation about the need for more vehicles that didn't seem to make sense, while every time I tried to interrupt, he went off into another flood of high Welsh oratory.

'For God's sake, see to it yourself!' I said in a rage.

As I left him, the adjutant touched my arm and, before I knew what was happening, I was up to my neck in what appeared to be a complaint from the other ranks on the subject of leave.

'Has everybody gone barmy round here?' I said wildly, but just at that moment Munro, who, as I'd pushed him aside, had done a quick dot-and-carry-one to the mess with his walking sticks working overtime, stuck his head out of the door and shouted.

'It's all richt the noo,' he yelled. 'Wheel him in!'

Whereupon the adjutant and Jones grabbed me by the arms and hurried me to the mess so fast my feet hardly touched the ground.

I couldn't believe my eyes, and saw at once what they'd all been up to, because, while they'd kept me busy, the rest of the squadron had been decorating the place from floor to ceiling with flags – union jacks, RAF flags, naval flags, signal flags, Belgian and French flags they'd borrowed, and even one or two German ones they'd turned up. Someone had lit candles all over the place, too, and with everybody standing grinning round a large birthday cake, above the bar I saw a sign, 'Happy Birthday.'

'Whose birthday is it?' I asked.

'Yours, ye damn' fuil,' Munro said and, as I remembered that it was, they all started singing.

I'm twenty-one today.
I'm twenty-one today.
I've got the key of the door—'

Grinning, I pushed them away. 'I'm not twenty-one,' I said. 'I'm twenty.'

'Och, dinnae fash yersel' aboot that,' Munro shouted. 'We'll none of us ever live another year, mon, and it isnae every squadron at the front that's got an infant as acting CO.'

He went round with a feeding bottle full of wine, sloshing it into glasses, and shouted for a toast.

'To the baby terror of the skies,' he said. 'Brat Falconer! Claims tae be only twenty but from the time he's been flyin' oot here he *must* be as old as Methuselah.'

It turned into a wild party with Munro holding a mock investiture to give me a birthday present of a huge medal they'd made, which consisted of what looked like the cog wheel off one of the lorries' gear boxes, painted like an RAF rondel and suspended on a foot wide 'ribbon' made of canvas and daubed in all the colours of the rainbow.

'Tae gae wi' the others,' he said. 'Well done, thou guid an' faithful sairvant,' and there were cheers and shouting and pieces of bread flying round. I don't think I ever enjoyed a birthday so much in my life.

As the major recovered and I found myself in the air again, the problem of survival took its place once more in the scheme of things. My generation was one which had almost forgotten what it was like for people to die peacefully, and faces were coming and going so fast I couldn't remember half of them. Things had changed in another direction, too, because for the first time comradeship began to wane. With the Germans reeling eastwards, everybody was making plans for after the war and their minds all seemed to be full of their families and their jobs. A few of us, however, hadn't been old enough to have jobs and to us the future was just a void because we couldn't conceive what it would be like or even whether we'd ever be able to settle to a steady workaday chore. The break-up of the whole world seemed to be near because the only thing I could remember was squadron life and, afraid suddenly, I clung closer to Munro who, although he was older than I was, at least seemed to belong to both worlds – the new world of careers and the old world of last year.

The sound of guns to the east nowadays came almost continuously, and with the Americans beginning to appear in greater numbers every day, none of us expected the war to go on longer than 1919. The spring offensives then ought to put paid to the Germans for good, we felt, and I just hoped I'd still be around to celebrate.

As the autumn arrived in cooler days and greyer skies, places we'd been trying to capture for four years fell at last and our job now seemed to consist only of chivvying the German infantry wherever they tried to stand, flying low into the murk of the greenish smoke of gas shells, dropping bombs and machine-gunning until I was sick of the narrow escapes and sick of the killing.

'Ah thought we were supposed tae be "birdmen",' Munro grumbled. 'Knights o' the air. That sort o' stuff. Most o' the time these days we're so low Ah'm looking up at the trees.'

Flying had become a cheerless chore far too close to the tainted earth, pouring our machines in and out of the valleys and lifting them over the rises in the land, dodging trees and houses and telegraph poles so that your heart spent most of its time in the region of your throat, choking you with a fright that was even worse when you were down and had time to think about it. It didn't make for sound sleep but a comforting worm of hope told me I might see it through, though the sight of Munro's haggard face was no help. A short spell of leave after his flu had convinced him it was time he got married and he'd actually got as far as popping the question. He'd returned in a seventh heaven of delight because Barbara Hatherley had said 'yes' to him, but he was terrified now that he'd never live to meet her at the altar.

'Thank heaven it'll soon be over,' he kept muttering.

Then I discovered to my horror that there were grey hairs in my head and I was so afraid it would all drop out and leave me bald I felt I had to write and tell Charley. She took a long time to answer because it seemed she, too, had been down with flu, but her letter was brisk and as cheerful as ever.

'My heart bleeds for you,' she wrote. 'But, though I've got some dark recesses in my soul, they've never been so dark I'd turn my back on a man just because he looked like a boiled egg.'

It made me hoot with laughter and, feeling nothing would ever change her, I decided she was the most wonderful girl in the world. She'd never pushed herself, never tried feminine wiles on me or made special demands. She was just amusing, full of courage, desperately alive and shiningly honest.

Then I thought again of Marie-Ange and as I wondered what had happened to her I began to wish I could get it all sorted out because I somehow didn't feel I was playing fair with Charley. She'd always been careful in her letters to avoid serious-ness but sometimes the care was so careful it seemed to show through, and I knew that occasionally she needed me around to cheer her up as I did her.

Again I decided I'd try to get a couple of days off to go to see her but again it didn't work out that way, because we were ordered further east once more, and from that time on we never seemed to stop. The Germans were moving backwards faster than we could move forward, because they were retreating into the clean undamaged land, while we were advancing across the battlefields and all the soiled, smashed countryside which they were booby-trapping and systematically destroying to delay us.

As we moved on, we never seemed to stop long enough to unpack properly, so that we lived in acute discomfort most of the time. Sleeping and eating arrangements were always bad, and the mess was never quite as it had been and certainly never as messes had been in 1917 and 1916. We were always short of men because half-trained youngsters straight from school kept coming out, some of, it seemed to me, with the look of death already on their faces, and after their first half-dozen trips were either dead or dead lucky and thanking God they'd lived long enough to learn something. Because we moved so fast replacements never seemed to come up, while the depot never seemed able to get spares and new machines to us when we needed them.

The long horror of the trenches seemed to have come to an end at last, though, and the armies were really on the move now. Tanks were pushing forward like ugly grey beetles, followed as often as not by cavalry, those solid phalanxes of lancers and swordsmen the generals had put their faith in ever since 1914 and never been able to use because they were hopeless in the mud or against barbed wire and machine guns. You felt you could almost see the smiles of satisfaction on the faces of the staff as they clattered past on the pavé, steel-helmeted Britishers and blue-turbanned Indians.

As we moved forward we began to come across the wreckage of machines lost months before, blackened and charred or simply stark silent debris with flags of fluttering fabric on the shattered wings. As often as not there was a grave beside them, sometimes even with a name that someone knew, and one day, as we set up shop near Meulebeke, a farmer came with an identity disc and a few personal possessions that belonged to Milne. His machine had fallen into the river, it seemed, and two days before some farmhand, trying for fish, had found his body in the reeds. Munro and I went to claim it, and while it was not recognizable as Milne it couldn't have been anybody else.

There were troops all round the aerodrome now, thousands of them: American and British; New Zealanders, Australians, South Africans, Canadians and Indians, the whole weight of the Empire, all moving forward, all flushed and excited at the possibility of victory. Occasionally the German bombers came, their unsynchronized Mercedes engines drumming, the crashes in the distance shaking the huts and making sleep impossible.

It began to grow colder and food became scarce because the Germans were grabbing everything ahead of us and probably hoping to take it home to their starving families. But the damage they left behind them didn't appear to be deliberate any longer – as though they were sick of the destruction, too – and no one took any notice of the stories of atrocities the newspapers still hopefully put out.

Then we found ourselves on an old German airfield in a mess still decorated with salvaged Lewises and the rondels and numbers of British machines. Photographs of former occupants who'd been killed still hung over the bar, and, as I had as a prisoner, I thought it was a funny way to decorate a mess. Munro was banging away on the piano and, because I was so tired, it was only then that I realized where we were.

I stood up with a jerk and stared round. I could still feel the cold wine of the previous year in the glass in my hand and could remember as though it were yesterday the stiff figures with high-collared tunics giving me jerky little bows. I looked round almost as though I could hear a German voice speaking in my ear.

'How old are you, Herr Hauptmann?'

'Nineteen.'

'You look twenty-six. It is the war.'

I swung on my heels, staring at the walls, almost as though I could see that small blond figure with the blue and white cross at his throat, older than I'd expected, as tired as I felt now and just as lacking in enthusiasm. Suddenly I knew how *he* must have felt.

Abruptly, I left the mess and went to the farm building where we were billeted to snatch up my map and smooth it out. There it was, as clear as day: Lambres. Tournai. Noyelles. I was still staring at it when Munro burst into the hut.

'Y'all right, laddie?' he demanded.

'Yes,' I said. 'I'm all right.'

'The way ye went oot, I though mebbe ye'd been taken sick.'

'No,' I said. 'I'm not sick. I'm fine.'

'Fine?' He gave me a quizzical look.

'Well, fairly fine.' I managed a grin. 'Like you, I expect.' I gestured. 'This is where I was shot down, Jock. I half-expected Krefft to walk in.'

'Who's Krefft?'

'The man who nabbed me. He'd been to school in England. He gave me a couple of books – to make captivity less boring, he said. There were some others: Pastor and Gontermann and Von der Osten. It was here I met Richthofen. He stood right where you were sitting at the piano. For a minute I thought I was looking at a ghost.'

Munro gave a wry grin. 'Me an' you, laddie, have been doin' naethin' else but look at ghosts for a long time.'

I jabbed at the map. 'It was there they shoved me in clink,' I went on. 'And that's where I met Sykes and where we got out and walked north.'

'Wi' yon gel?'

'Yes,' I said. 'Jock, I've got to find out what became of her.'

He frowned. 'I always haird it was no' a guid thing tae gae back on y'r tracks, laddie. I always haird that things never seem the same. Hills that ye thought were high as a child turrn oot tae be only pimples, an' people ye thought were beautiful turrn oot tae be just naethin' but plain. Ye don't question much when ye're young.'

'I wasn't young, Jock,' I said. 'I'd done two, nearly three, tours in France by that time. And that made me as old as any man alive. I knew what I was doing then and I know what I'm doing now. I'm going to find her.'

'The war's still on, laddie,' he pointed out gently.

I shrugged. 'Then for twenty-four hours or so,' I said, 'it'll have to do without me.'

Chapter 7

It was raining just as it had been the year before, blowing in flurries against the windscreen of the major's tender, which I'd borrowed without asking.

By this time, I thought, he'd be wondering where it had gone, and would probably be asking himself whether I'd been taken sick, deserted or simply gone off my chump. I'd decided he could wait to find out, though, and that my reputation was good enough to get me past any enquiries that might be made, and had just tossed on my old leather flying coat without buttoning it and gone.

With the aid of my map I had no difficulty finding the place. I'd had no idea it was called *Ferme des Quatre Vents* but, then, on my last visit the previous year I'd never gone to the gate to see the name on the post except after dark. The place didn't seem to have changed much except that there was a hole in the roof that looked as though it had

191

been made by a shell or a bomb, there were no cattle, and the barn looked a little lopsided as if it had been caught by blast.

When I pulled the car to a halt at the front, I realized it had been taken over by a battery of heavy guns. The great weapons were dug in behind the orchard and a couple of officers were sitting in the armchairs I'd last seen occupied by Marie-Ange and her mother. The barn where Sykes and I had hidden was jammed with gunners. They'd erected bunks like shelves from floor to roof and were sleeping, reading, writing letters, washing, shaving, and repairing their clothes at every level.

'Something we can do for you, old boy?' one of the officers asked.

'Yes,' I said. 'I'm looking for the family.'

'What family?'

'The family that lived here. I was here last year.'

'Couldn't have been, old boy. Must have got the wrong place. The Germans were here then.'

'So was I,' I insisted. 'In that damn' barn. I'd just escaped from prison.'

The officer, who was about my age, gave a whistle. 'Such fun,' he commented mildly. 'Hide here?'

'They hid us.'

'Well, I'm sorry, old fruit, but there's nobody here now. There was nobody here when we arrived and we just took it over. Used the top of the wind-mill for an observation post.'

'There were two of them. Mother and daughter. Know what happened to them?'

'There's a grave in the orchard. Would that be 'em? Name of De Camaerts, I think.'

He led me round the back of the house and showed me the crude wooden cross that had been erected. The name on it wasn't *Marie-Ange*, however. It was *Giselle-Marie* and, judging by the age and the date, I guessed it must have been her mother.

I wondered if the shell that had gone through the roof and knocked the barn sideways had killed her, or whether – because she was pretty frail – she'd just died. And then I wondered who'd buried her and if it had been Marie-Ange and what heartbreak she'd gone through.

'What happened to the other one?' I asked. 'Any idea?'

'Not the foggiest, old son. I can ask about, if you like.'

'No—' I had another idea – 'I think I know where I might find out.'

Leaving the officers sitting in their chairs drinking tea, I drove to Noyelles. The place was full of allied troops now, as it had been full of men in field grey then, and the guns and the horses and the shouts and jeers as they passed were in English instead of German. They were going by in a steady stream towards the east, guns, lorries, horses, men, jamming the narrow streets and scraping great scars on the shoddy red-brick buildings that hung over the roadway. They were moving forward this time with a sureness and a certainty that I'd never seen before and for the first time I knew that the war really was ending.

The *maire* was in his office in the red-brick *mairie*, probably the first time he'd sat in it since the Germans had originally occupied it in 1914. He knew what had happened.

'The mother lived alone there, monsieur,' he said. 'When we heard she died, I got permission from the Germans to go out and bury her. We dug the grave in the orchard.'

'And the daughter?'

'I don't know, Monsieur. I heard the Germans arrested her and took her away.'

My heart heavy in my chest, I thanked him and left. There was still one more place.

It took me about thirty minutes to get to Lambres near Roubaix and another ten to find the centre of the town and the headquarters of the town major. It hadn't changed much since I'd last seen it, just the union jack instead of the black, red and yellow of the German flag. There were guards outside still, though they wore khaki this time instead of grey, and it had the same look of smart super-efficiency you always found around headquarters, bases, dumps, and all the other places where the stress lay less on fighting than organization, spit and polish. Perhaps they'd just taken it over as it was, lock, stock and barrel, tables, chairs, discipline, everything.

The town major wasn't in his room as I put my head round the door, but for a moment the walls seemed to ring with those words that had so frightened me the previous year: That I would be *sofort totgeschossen* – shot dead at once – if I tried to escape.

Without asking anyone if I could, I found my way up the stairs and on the next floor stopped outside a door. That hadn't changed either, but the room beyond was empty this time, except for what looked like the same two iron bedsteads we'd used to make our escape and the same two straw-filled sacking mattresses. I went straight to the corner of the room and read the pencilled inscription on the peeling whitewash – '*Abandon hope all ye who enter here.*' It had been there the previous autumn when I'd been there. I looked further along for the list of names. *Lieutenant, F Holben, RA; Captain FJH Carter, Warwicks; Lieutenant Hawkins, G, Lancashire Fusiliers.* They were still there – a whole string of them – longer now than it had been when I'd seen it last – and there, bang in the middle, were *Captain M Falconer, RFC and Major CLWBD Sykes*, 12th Lancers and RFC.

I was still staring at them, feeling as if I'd moved back in time, when I heard a footstep on the landing. I whirled round, scared and half expecting to see a spiked helmet, but it was just a plump fat-faced lieutenant with pink cheeks, a well-brushed uniform, a provost officer's armband, light-coloured breeches, polished riding boots you could see your face in and the air of someone with a little authority who thought a great deal of himself. He belonged with those smart, officious young men at the pilots' pool at Berck and it stuck out a mile that he'd only recently come to the front and was trying hard to look martial.

He took one look at the back of the unfastened smelly leather coat I wore, staring down his nose at all its oilstains and the absence of rank badges, and I saw his pink cheeks grow pinker still with indignation. People who looked like I did clearly had no part in the tight little unit he ran.

'What the hell are you doing in here?' he asked. 'This is the detention room!'

'I'd call it a cell,' I said.

'Never mind what it is! What do you want?'

I shrugged. 'Just to have a look at it. I once spent a night in here.'

He stared at me as though I were some old sweat who'd been picked up drunk in the gutter, and took another look at my coat. 'I can imagine,' he said. 'It must have been before we got here.'

'Not half it wasn't,' I said. 'When I was in this cell the Germans were still here and your opposite number was a fat chap like you with a spiked helmet who threatened to shoot me dead.'

'Who the devil are you calling "fat"?' he exploded. 'I'll have you know, my good fellow, that I'm acting town major!'

'And I'm Charlie Chaplin's half-brother,' I said. I jabbed aggressively at the whitewash. 'That's my name – Falconer—' I jabbed again – 'and that's the name of the chap who shared the cell with me.' Then for the first time I turned completely round, leather coat flying, and glared at him. 'And don't call me "your good fellow" because, as it happens, if I take this coat off you'll see I'm senior to you in rank and a great deal older, I'll bet, in terms of active service!'

As he saw the string of ribbons I'd collected, he blushed and saluted and began to bluster, until he looked just like the elderly German who'd threatened to shoot me the year before in that very same building, and I reflected there were just as many stuffed dummies in our army as there were in the German. And as I watched him slapping and stamping and generally thrashing about like a stranded whale in an effort to make up for putting his foot in it, I even found I liked it, and decided that I must be growing bad-tempered and malicious enough in my old age actively to enjoy other people's discomfort. Or perhaps it was just impatience with people who were playing at being soldiers. Either that or else there was something developing inside me that would one day make one of those senior officers Sykes said I ought to be, all fuss, feathers and fury, because for someone only just twenty I was doing pretty well.

'How long were you here, sir?' Fatface was all obsequiousness and concern now, trying to make amends.

'One day,' I said.

'Not long, sir.'

'Long enough, but there was a chap in here at the time who had a few bright ideas.' And who was a sight better man than you are, too, I thought.

He shuffled his feet and tried again to be friendly, frightened I'd court-martial him or something, I supposed. 'How did you get out, sir?' he asked.

I jerked a hand at the tiny window, set in a deep recess high up on the wall. 'Through there.'

He stared, as though he didn't believe me, and perhaps he didn't because we'd had to reach it by using one of the beds as a ladder and climbing up without our boots, with our toes in the springs, and we'd made a rope of our scarves to lower ourselves to the roof outside. After that we'd scrambled down God alone knew how many more roofs before we'd finally dropped to the ground in the dungheap of the stables and bolted.

'You got all the records for this place?' I asked. 'The German records?'

'Yes, sir,' he said. 'They took off so fast we captured the lot.'

'Arrests and everything?'

'I think so.'

'Do you read German?'

'No.' I hadn't expected he would.

'Anybody who does?'

'There's a sergeant downstairs, sir.'

'Get him. Fast.'

I was being horrifyingly rude to him but, if the boot had been on the other foot, I know he would have been even worse to me and I hadn't the graciousness of Sykes and people like him. He reappeared shortly afterwards, spraying 'sirs' round the room like a garden hose, and produced a sergeant with a batch of ledgers.

'Arrests,' I said. 'You got my name down there?'

The sergeant found it in no time. There obviously hadn't been all that many prisoners lodged there.

'How about civilians?' I asked.

'There are a few, sir.'

'Women?'

'Three, sir.'

'One of 'em De Camaerts? Marie-Ange de Camaerts?'

He lifted up his head and stared at me as though I were clairvoyant. 'How did you know, sir?'

'Never mind how I know. What happened to her?'

The sergeant ran his finger over the spiky German handwriting. 'Accused of helping British prisoners to escape, sir.'

'That was me. Go on.'

The sergeant looked up, his face set in an expression of sorrow. 'Sentenced to death, sir.'

My heart felt like stone. 'When?'

'Last year, sir.'

'Where is she buried?'

'Sir—' the sergeant was still busy reading '—I think she probably isn't dead. The sentence was commuted to imprisonment during the governor's pleasure.'

'Which prison? Come on, man, quick.'

'Fort Ralas, sir.'

'Where is it?'

'Douai, sir.'

'Are they all still there?'

'No, sir. We freed everybody when we arrived.'

'Then where is she now?'

The sergeant peered at the ledgers and turned over a few pages while I fidgeted impatiently.

'It says here, sir, that she was transferred to hospital two months back, sir. In August.'

'Which one?'

'Hôpital de Sainte Marie de Douleur. At Douai, sir. It's one we took over when we arrived.'

'You sure?'

'Yes, sir.'

I swung round on Fatface. 'Telephone 'em,' I said. 'See if she's still there.'

He jumped for the telephone as though the hounds of hell were after him. I still hadn't taken off my leather coat and he probably thought from the way I was acting that I was at least a colonel – probably even one of the boy brigadiers the war had thrown up. I decided I'd learned a lot in three years.

There was a lot of talk over the telephone because the hospital seemed to be as hidebound as the army and there seemed to be a lot of people there like the staff at Berck and Army HQ, who seemed more concerned with following the rules than getting anything done, but at last his face changed and he seemed to be getting somewhere.

'Yes,' he said. 'That's correct. De Camaerts, Marie-Ange.' He looked up at me and I nodded quickly. 'That sounds as though it could be her,' he went on. 'Have you her address? Where? Rue de la Paix, Lille. You sure? There's another address? Ferme des Quatre Vents?'

I signalled wildly that that was enough. I didn't want her life history. I knew that already.

He put down the telephone, flushed with success. 'I think I've found her, sir,' he said.

'Right,' I said. 'Where is this hospital?'

'Just off the Grande Place, sir,' the sergeant volunteered.

'Anyone there will tell you, I imagine,' Fatface said. 'There's a military policeman in the middle of the square. He must direct ambulances in and out of the place a couple of dozen times a day.'

'Right. Thank you.' I was thawing out a little, so that he wouldn't think all senior officers were stinkers.

'You've been very kind.'

He actually blushed with pleasure – probably expecting at least a DSO – then, as I swung away, he coughed and called after me.

'Sir!'

I stopped and turned.

'They say she's been very ill, sir.'

My heart sank again. For some reason it had never occurred to me that she'd been transferred to the hospital as a patient. Somehow I'd thought only that she'd been sent there to do menial tasks as part of her punishment, because the Germans had always rounded up civilians in occupied territory and put them to work for them.

'What was wrong with her?' I said quietly.

'It seems she had the Spanish influenza like so many other people.'

'Go on.' I knew there was more.

'It turned to pneumonia and, with the Germans more concerned at the time with retreating than looking after people, it became rather a bad dose, sir. I gather she came pretty close to—'

'Right,' I said quickly. 'Never mind. And thank you again.'

Fatface slammed up into a salute that would have done credit to a guardsman as I swept out. I suspect that afterwards he flopped into his chair and said 'Phew!' But he'd done his stuff. With a firework under his behind, he seemed to know how to go about things.

I drove to Douai like a lunatic, threading in and out of the traffic. Several times soldiers I jostled to the ditches shouted out angrily at me and once a military policeman ordered me to pull into a side road to allow a battery of field guns to go past. I ignored them all, slipping under the tossing heads of the gun teams and round the backs of lorries smelling of hot oil. Once a red-tabbed officer bawled furiously at me because I pushed in front of him but I decided that if he'd made a note of the number on the car he'd be able to sort it all out with the major when I returned it. I had a feeling that the major would back me up, too, because he didn't have much time for red tabs either. Though he'd probably be biting the carpet about the car being missing – especially if he'd been intending to use it for something himself – I felt sure he wouldn't let me down.

Fatface was right about the policeman. There he was, standing in the middle of the Grande Place directing the traffic as if he were in Piccadilly. And he *did* know where the hospital was. Five minutes later I had left the car outside the door and was arguing fiercely with the English nurse in charge of admissions. She didn't want to let me in because, she said, visiting wasn't permitted. I told her I wasn't leaving until I'd seen whom I'd come to see and that if she were difficult I'd just stamp in, anyway.

In the end, she got on the telephone and rang someone up and five minutes later the sister, an older woman with a kinder face, appeared.

'The civilian part of the hospital has nothing to do with us,' she said. 'We have no authority over it at all.'

'Look, sister,' I begged. 'I have to see this girl. Can't you arrange it for me?'

She gave me a long curious look. 'Does she mean a lot to you?' she asked.

'I don't know,' I said. 'Not yet. I only know that when I was taken prisoner with my major by the

Germans last year it was entirely due to her that we managed to escape. They tell me the Germans found out what she did and imprisoned her for it. She caught influenza and it's been a life and death case for a bit. When we escaped I didn't have the chance to say thank you to her but I always promised I'd come back. Well, I've come back and, whatever happens to her, she's got to know I've come back.'

She studied me for a while then she nodded. 'The doctor in charge is a kind man,' she said. 'He's a Belgian and he's grateful for what we've done. I think matron might be able to arrange something. Just wait here.'

I waited for what seemed hours, watched curiously by the nurse, then the sister came back with a Belgian soldier who limped and used a stick.

'The orderly will take you to the nurse in charge of the ward,' the sister said. 'I think it'll be all right.'

She was still watching me curiously as I went off after the limping orderly. Despite his bad leg he moved fast and we walked down what seemed miles of corridors. The British army had taken over the best part of the hospital for the wounded and the civilians had all been pushed into temporary quarters at the back, and we climbed stairs and crossed lawns and eventually arrived at the entrance to a hut. A Belgian nun with a wide-winged head-dress was waiting for us.

'*S'il vous plaît*,' she said, indicating a door.

The ward was big and bleak and bare, as though the Germans had stolen everything worth stealing, and there was a squat stove in the centre with an iron guard round it and a few women patients sitting knitting and sewing. Curious faces stared at me from pillows as I clattered down the ward, then the nun pulled a screen aside.

'*Enfin!*' I heard her say softly. '*Il arrive!*'

As Munro had suggested, Marie-Ange wasn't as beautiful as I'd remembered her. Even allowing for her wasted frame and pale sunken face, I knew at once that I'd been seeing her through rose-pink spectacles ever since the previous year. As I sat down on the chair the nun pushed forward, I saw her head turn. There was a curious calm in her face that I thought might be the approach of death and her eyes were huge and black against her pallid cheeks.

'*L'aviateur aux grands pieds*,' she murmured, and at first I couldn't think what she meant. Then I remembered the huge farm boots she'd found for me to wear in place of my flying boots, and the way she'd pulled my leg about them.

'*Oui.*' I lifted my foot. '*La même chose exactement.*'

Her pale lips moved and she managed a twisted smile, then her hand moved across the bedspread and grasped mine as I put it out.

'You came back,' she said.

Chapter 8

The major was sympathetic when I got back, and I began to realize that because I'd been so long at the front they were all giving me special treatment. He just waved his hand when I told him why I'd taken his car and asked if I'd found what I was looking for.

'Yes, sir,' I said. 'I think she's probably dying.'

'Like a day or two off flying?' he asked. 'To sort things out. It can be arranged.'

'It would help,' I said. 'I think I – we – all of us – owe it to them.'

'I think so, too,' he agreed. 'There must be dozens of people like her and if nothing else it'll be good for Belgian–British relations.'

He even lent me a motor bike and sidecar so I could move about as I pleased. I was glad of that because I also felt I ought to go and see Charley and tell her how things had turned out. She'd always been interested in Marie-Ange.

She seemed surprisingly poised as she came to meet me. It was a warm day and she led me out into the grounds where we could talk without being overheard.

'I think she's been waiting all this time for me to come back, Charley,' I said uneasily. 'What ought I to do?'

'Go back,' she said at once.

'I've *been*.'

'Well, *keep on* going. Until she's better.'

'Suppose she—' I paused '—suppose she's expecting, well, what you suggested.'

'Marriage?' She chuckled. 'I'll be a bridesmaid, if you like.'

I glared at her. She didn't seem to be discussing what seemed to be a serious matter in anything like the right spirit. I felt about sixteen and like a schoolboy caught out in a misdemeanour. It would have done Fatface good to have seen me just then.

'I wish you'd stop being an ass, Charley,' I said irritably.

She was still studying me with an amused light in her eye. 'When are you going to pop the question?' she asked.

'Pop the question? I'm not.'

'What if she expects it?'

I felt trapped, as though things were closing in around me. I hadn't expected to pop the question to anybody for a long time yet.

Charley smiled. 'You have the look of a man condemned to death,' she said.

I turned to look at her. She seemed terribly adult all at once and I realized suddenly that all those old affectations of hers had been gone for some time. Her enthusiasm was still as great as ever but it was under control now and her voice was no longer the unrestrained yelp of an excited girl but the quieter, more confident address of someone who was bewilderingly mature.

'I don't really want to get married yet, Charley,' I said slowly, 'and when I do, I'd begun to think perhaps, well—'

She studied me calmly. 'Spit it out, old thing,' she said.

I'd realized for ages now that just being with Charley, just walking with her, made me feel alive because she was invariably warm, satisfying and eager without archness, as though it were the most natural thing in the world that we should enjoy being together. She'd always made me feel the cleverest chap in the world, and when we'd held hands, as we did occasionally – not with sentimentality, but because we were happy – it had slowly become an unconscious caress that I'd barely noticed because it had become so normal, and the idea had been growing in me for a long time that what lay between us had become something a lot deeper than friendship.

She was still waiting for an explanation.

'Charlotte—'

She looked startled. 'Pardon!'

I frowned. 'I said, "Charlotte"—'

'My word!' Her smile was gently mocking. 'We are serious, aren't we! You've never called me *that* before.'

'Well, I am doing now,' I snapped, not wishing to be interrupted at what seemed a portentous moment in my career. 'We've known each other a long time—'

'Who have—?'

She didn't seem to be responding properly to the cues.

'Charley,' I fumed. 'Shut up!'

'Sorry.'

There was a pause while I drew another deep breath, 'I've always thought a lot about you—'

Her temper flared. 'No, you didn't, you fibber!' she said hotly. 'There *was* a time even when you thought I was about the stupidest girl in England.'

My jaw dropped. 'Charley, I didn't—'

'Yes, you did!' Her face was pink with chagrin. 'Ludo told me I hadn't a chance.'

'Did you ask him?'

'Yes. And he told me what you said when he made a few discreet enquiries on my behalf.' She stared at me, her eyes frank and honest. 'And you were probably right, too, because all I can remember thinking about in those days – years ago—'

'Last year.'

'That's years ago these days, isn't it? All I thought about then were clothes and tea-dances and the latest fad and the newest hairstyles. I must have bored you to tears.'

I grinned. 'You did a bit at times. Not much, though, and never now. You've changed.'

'It must be the war,' she said wonderingly. 'It does things to people.' She grinned, suddenly enjoying herself. 'Do go on. You were just beginning to sound interesting.'

I hesitated then blundered on again. 'Well – I hadn't thought – not yet, of course, because, well, there's a long way to go—'

'But you want someone to cherish you and all that rot, but you don't want to be tied down too much. Is that it?'

She was gazing at me with the clearest of blue eyes. I stared back at her, startled at her perception, then I gave a sheepish grin. 'I suppose that's about it. Because I've got to decide what I'm going to do when the war's over first.'

She gave me a sly look. 'Suppose someone else comes along?' she asked. 'Someone who's a bit older than you. Twenty-one, say. Suppose he asked me? Hospital makes them sentimental.'

'It *does*?' I gaped at her. 'What do you do?'

'Take violent evasive action. It's the nurse's uniform, y'see. It does things for a girl. Makes her even seem attractive.'

'You *are* attractive.'

'Go on! I've got a face like a horse.'

'No you haven't.'

'*And* a loud voice. It's a bray, I think, really. Happens to all well-bred girls from county families. Comes from going to too many horse-shows.'

'Charley, I think you're terrific.'

She beamed. 'Honest?'

'Yes. But I've got to get a career first because I haven't a bean.'

'That makes two of us. Neither have I.'

'I thought the Sykeses had plenty of money.'

'Not *our* branch of the family. *We're* as poor as church mice. All we've got is a family tree that goes so far back it disappears into the mists of time, and a house that was built in the eighteenth century, neglected in the nineteenth, and started to fall down in this one, because we'd no money to keep it up. All that and an inbred snobbishness that enables us to go on thinking that, despite everything, it's still worth the proletariat's while to get hitched to us.'

I grinned. 'It is.'

She studied me cautiously. 'Sure you're not letting yourself be carried away a bit?'

'No,' I said. Actually, I was, because I'd never really intended to tell her what I thought of her — not for years — for the simple reason that I couldn't afford to, and I'd thought it best kept to myself until the right time. But it was out now, and that was that, and I found I didn't mind.

Charley didn't seem to mind either. Quite the opposite, in fact, because she was blushing like mad suddenly and with all her poise gone. 'Sorry I pulled your leg,' she said. 'Actually, it's rather spiffing, and I'm pleased as anything.'

'You are?'

'Why not?' she said. 'I can't think of anyone I admire more. And that's important, isn't it? And what's more—' she tapped the medal ribbons I wore '—when this stupid war's over you're not the type to go round living on those things. You're a nasty stubborn type, Martin Falconer, and even though you still always manage to fall over the carpet every time you come into a room, I dare bet my savings, which aren't much, heaven knows, that twenty years from now you'll *be* someone.'

'Think so?'

'I'm sure.' She smiled at me. 'You know, I never thought you'd get around to it – in spite of the hints I kept dropping.'

'*Did* you drop hints?'

'Like mad. I had a terrible crush on you. I even kept all the letters you wrote. Tied up with blue ribbon at the bottom of a drawer. Soppy as anything.'

A slow smile spread across my face. This was a Charley I didn't know and I felt flattered, because I'd never done much to deserve such devotion. Charley was looking at me, shy for the first time since I'd known her. 'I'm glad you finally caught on,' she said.

I kissed her. Same as always, except that this time it seemed rather more important and we were a little less perfunctory. It went very well, I thought, though our noses got in the way at first, and this time, too, she put her arms round me and hugged me. As she released me, her eyes were sparkling and I wasn't sure if it weren't with tears. I grinned at her, not knowing what to say because it seemed such a big step to take, even though it was still only in the planning stage, and we both still seemed a bit young for it.

'Ludo always said you'd marry a duke,' I pointed out.

She chuckled. 'By the time we've managed to save enough money,' she said, 'you'll probably *be* a duke.'

We stared at each other a moment longer, neither of us knowing what to say next, then I took a deep breath. 'That's it then,' I said. 'We'll just have to wait a bit, that's all.'

'There's just one thing,' she said, suddenly sober and solemn and all the smiles gone from her face.

'What's that?'

'You've forgotten Marie-Ange de Camaerts. I think that's what you came to tell me about, isn't it? Not your suddenly discovered affection for me.'

–

It worried me all the way back to the squadron. I realized now that Marie-Ange hadn't really meant all that much to me. I'd admired her and been deeply in her debt for what she'd done for us, but now, thinking about it, I could only put it down to youthful sentiment. Sykes and I had been cold, tired, hungry, miserable and frightened of being stuck in a great wire cage somewhere in Germany for years, and the fact that she'd taken pity on us and helped us to safety had made me see her as a sort of Joan of Arc in shining armour. I think I'd fallen for a funny accent and the way she wrinkled her nose when she laughed at my leg-pulling, and, looking back on myself as I'd been the year before from the enormous height of twenty, I was able to see myself as a callow youth a mere nineteen years old, shy, over-emotional, easily impressed, and just a bit silly.

It continued to worry me, though, and there was plenty of time for it to develop because when I went to see Marie-Ange again several days had passed and there had been a lot of fighting. By now it really did seem that we were out to win the war and nothing else. No nonsense about pushing out a salient or nipping off a bulge. Victory was the aim now, as certain as it was that the sun would rise the next morning, and we were already reaching out towards Sedan, and the French civilians near the airfield were almost speechless with joy at the liberation they'd almost ceased to hope for.

The Germans were by no means driven from the sky, however. They were as vicious as they'd ever been, as though their air force, which had not been born before the war, was determined that if it were to die after the war, it was at least going to leave the scene with some honour.

The second time Marie-Ange looked less worn and even a little better but the nun still warned me I wasn't to tire her. She didn't seem to want to talk, however, and just grasped my hand in silence.

'I was sorry to find out about your mother,' I said.

'Yes,' she agreed. 'She was very old and very fragile.' Then she promptly went to sleep, so that I just sat there staring at her, my mind full of bewilderment.

The nun put her head in from time to time and beamed at us understandingly, as if she knew exactly how I was feeling, and once she even brought the mother superior.

'*Qu'elle est belle,*' she said. '*Et Monsieur le capitaine, qu'il est héroïque.*'

When she'd gone I took another look at Marie-Ange. She wasn't *really* beautiful – any more than I was heroic – and the thought worried me all the way back to the squadron as I tried to decide what love was. Was it familiarity, acceptance, easiness, comfort, a whole lot of ordinary-sounding emotions that went to make up something more? Or was it what everyone said it was, what all the novelists and song writers made it out to be? As I wondered if you could live with someone for the rest of your life without having to feel they were the most beautiful girl in the world, I began to think of the song that Munro was always pounding out on the mess piano.

> And when I tell them
> How wonderful you are,
> They'll never believe me—

Life wasn't a bit like that, I decided, and I thought of people who couldn't all have been married to beautiful or handsome people. I'd never thought of my father as being particularly good-looking and I knew I wasn't, and I don't think my mother was ever particularly beautiful. She'd probably been pretty when she'd been young and she still had a strange fey charm about her, but that wasn't the same. Yet they'd seemed to have lived happily together, and I knew it wouldn't somehow be the same with Marie-Ange.

The weather was awful now, with mist and flurries of rain, and we were all hoping they'd stop us flying, but it seemed essential that the war went on to the bitter bloody end so that we lost three men – all newcomers – in as many days. One dead, one wounded and one with his jaw broken in a crash-landing.

'I thought the damn' war was o'er,' Munro said bitterly. 'Do yon fools at Wing want tae kill us all tae prove it?'

But the flying still went on and the losses went on until we were all shaken, sullen and a little bewildered. If the war were about to end there seemed no point in getting us all killed. But that seemed to be the policy and, by now, apart from Munro and Jones and the major, there seemed to be no one left in the mess I knew, while those who had gone I could only remember after they'd been dimmed by the gentleness of memory so that they all seemed to have been brave and true and good – which I'm sure they weren't.

By this time the continued low flying had brought my nerves to bowstring tightness and I was doing the work with a numb indifference that was dangerous. I'd ceased to care and that, I knew, was the worst time of all, and I knew I was lethargic with fatigue and growing edgy because, while I'd never imagined I could be killed in an aeroplane, now I was beginning to think luck might just be against me for once. Because I seemed to have been flying in battle half my life, I was terrified that I'd been doing it just too long.

There was one blessed day of relief when it rained and I took the opportunity to go to Douai again. By this time it was well behind the line and not so full of fighting troops, and the stores people and the headquarters clerks and the lines of communications troops were much more in evidence. I was feeling so low I even made my peace with Fatface, buying a bottle of the best wine I could find at an officers' store and taking it in to him. He was so overcome he could barely speak.

I didn't stay and drove out to the hospital between all the hurrying people. The nurse at the entrance didn't argue any more and simply picked up the telephone. The same limping orderly arrived and led me down the endless corridors. The Belgian nun escorted me without speaking down the ward to the screen and because she said nothing I began to fear the worst, and all the old bugaboos of what Marie-Ange might be expecting of me rose up again. Then I thought perhaps she really was dying now and that made me feel even worse because I considered it was my fault for escaping and leaving her behind to face the music.

But as we reached the screen and the nun pulled the curtain back I was startled by the improvement in her. This time she was half-sitting up, propped on pillows with a bunch of letters in her hand, and was clearly much better. Something had happened and the nun knew it too.

'*Quel change!*' she said gaily. '*Elle a récouvré la santé. C'est miraculeux, n'est-ce pas? Maintenant elle se porte bien et avec beaucoup de nourriture, dans une quinzaine elle demandera les souliers de danse.*'

Marie-Ange looked up at me and smiled and her nose wrinkled so that I realized just why I'd managed to fall so heavily for her the year before.

'You understand the words she say?' she asked.

'No,' I said. 'Not all of them. She went a bit fast.'

'She say, "What a change. I have recovered the health and it is a miracle because I am become well once more. With much nourishment, in a fifteen-day I will be asking for the shoes of the dance".'

'Dance shoes,' I corrected.

'So – the dance shoes.'

The change was so wonderful my worries disappeared and I felt as happy as she did.

'I was much pleased to see you come,' she said.
'All the time I am in the prison I know you will, of
course. I want you to. I much look forward to it.'

I hadn't the heart to tell her I'd almost forgotten
her in that time. 'And now you are back,' she
went on. 'When the war is over, we will have the
wedding.'

'The wedding?'

'*Mais oui. Le mariage.*'

'Oh!'

She was rushing things a little, I thought. 'Whose
wedding?' I asked nervously, all the worries coming
back.

'But, mine. As soon as I am well. You must be
there, of course.'

'Of course.' She had it all planned, it seemed.
'But when I came last time, you were so ill—'

'Much has happened.' Her eyes were bright. She
was still pale but it was quite clear she was on the
road to recovery now. 'I wait for much time and
then he comes back.'

Yes, I thought, and now he's wondering what the hell he's going to tell Charley.

'I think I shall never see him again,' she went on, 'and then suddenly he appears. From the nowhere. He has much medals. He is an officer. Everybody will be so pleased and I shall be so much proud.'

'Yes,' I said again.

'We shall have the colonel to come. And the English Major Sykes. And all the comrades. We shall be married here and eventually go back to the farm. My father's factory is free also from the Germans now and we shall be able to make the machines for sewing and have money again. He will be able to take over from my father who grows old and we shall keep the farm for the eggs and the milk and the week-end in the country.'

I hadn't really thought of running a sewing machine factory and I didn't even see myself much as a farmer.

'And you will be the – what do you call it – the most good man—'

But of course. The bridegroom always was the most good man.

She was wrinkling her brows, not satisfied with her English. 'Not the "most good" man,' she said. 'Good, better, most better. How do you say it?'

'Best,' I said. 'Best man—' I stared and then I almost shouted the words '—*best man!*'

'That is right.' She laughed gaily. 'The man who is the most important next to the bridegroom. He stand alongside to clutch the ring.'

Suddenly the whole atmosphere changed. I'd got it all wrong. 'Who're you marrying, Marie-Ange?' I asked.

'*Mais Hyacinthe,*' she said. 'You will recall Hyacinthe?' Then I remembered the Belgian boy she'd been keen on who'd gone away and who she'd thought was dead.

'The chap with the funny name?' I said.

'Théophile Hyppolite Hyacinthe d'Ydewalle is not a funny name,' she said sternly.

It seemed funny to me. 'You thought it was funny last year,' I pointed out.

She gave a shrug, as Gallic a one as you could get. 'Last year I am frightened and a little stupid. Last year I think he is just a nice boy, that is all. Now I know he is a fine man. He has been very brave and is *très bien décoré* like you. I shall be Madame d'Ydewalle.' She gave a little giggle. 'I tell him about you and how you hide at the farm. I tell him also your name. He laughs but I think he is much jealous. You know what he say?'

'What?'

'*Quel drôle nom!*'

'Funny name? Mine? Why?' It had never seemed funny to me, or, to my knowledge, to anybody else either.

'He speaks good English,' she said. 'More good than me. He knows many words. *Un grand vocabulaire.* He say, "But he has the name of two birds!" And "How strange the father must be, to give his son the name of two birds".'

'Two birds! Me?' Then the light dawned. 'Oh! Martin – Falconer! Of course!' Suddenly the day which had started out being so awful was full of cheer. 'You know,' I said, 'when I first arrived and you started talking about marriage I thought—'

She gazed at me solemnly. 'You thought—?'

'Yes, I thought – well, it was silly really—'

'You thought I mean *you* – you think I – *oh là là!*' She giggled. 'I cannot marry *you.* I am only eighteen.'

'You told me *last year* you were eighteen. That makes you nineteen now.'

She pulled a face. 'Perhaps then I am – what do you say—'

'Too enthusiastic?'

'Yes. And you are so old—'

'*Me!* Old!'

'—and you are the "hot stuff" pilot.'

I grinned, remembering the word we'd always used.

'And, so, you see,' she went on, 'I *must* marry Hyacinthe. Also, of course, he asks me first.'

The nun shooed me out soon afterwards, saying that Marie-Ange had had enough excitement for one day. I didn't argue and left happily, hardly touching the floor with relief, but still a little disturbed that Marie-Ange should think me so ancient. Since Krefft had thought so too, however, I decided there must be something in it and that the war had left a few marks on me so that, like Fatface, she'd assumed I was years older than I was. All the same it was wonderful to see her beginning to recover and to know that her future was assured, because she deserved no less for her courage and patriotism. But I could also see her now as a good Belgian housewife, wearing black on Sunday, and sitting in her parlour surrounded by the photographs of all her relatives. It was what she was intended for and it was right that it should be that way, and she'd known all along that what I'd felt the previous year was nothing more than sentiment and loneliness and perhaps a bit of fear. I could even remember her words. 'This is not a true thing,' she had said, 'when the Germans have gone and I see Belgian boys again I will not think so much about you, and when you see English girls you will also feel different.'

She'd been right and I felt as if the weight of the world had been lifted from my back. Somehow I had to get to St Marion the next day to tell Charley what had happened.

Chapter 9

I reckoned without the war. When I got back the major called me into his office, heard my news, laughed and congratulated me on my escape.

'Shouldn't think you'd really enjoy being a Belgian,' he said. 'All that olive oil.'

'The beer's awful, too,' I said.

He grinned, then his face became sombre again. 'All the same, I'm glad it's all settled,' he said, 'because we need you. The powers that be are demanding the full treatment. We're going to be busy. Starting tomorrow.'

Sure enough it all began again the next morning and in forty-eight hours Marie-Ange, even Charley, had slipped from my mind. Despite the weather, there was no pause and we went at it from dawn to dark in a driving endless round in the late autumn mist, hammering at the retreating Germans, shooting up their aerodromes, smashing their transport, killing their horse and mule teams, forcing them off the road and out of every battered red-brick house where they tried to stand. By the end of the week we were all taut-faced with the strain, but there was no halting and not much sleep because the next morning at dawn it started all over again in the same grinding terrifying chore that left us all limp, exhausted and shaking.

To stop the complaints, a batch of decorations all round arrived – including a posthumous one for Bull.

'Fat lot of good that is,' I said.

Sometimes, I began to think, I could hear Bullo's bell tolling myself, because we couldn't hope to keep up what we were doing for much longer. I was even beginning to dread flying by this time because there'd been too many near misses and I couldn't face the possibility of another. It wasn't that I'd lost the love of it – sometimes I longed simply to go up alone and ride on the upper air without fear – it was just that I was getting too much of it and at too low an altitude. Courage, as the air force doctors had found out, was something that wore out, and every time some madman's wing tips scraped past, every time a spattering of bullets holed the wings, or I limped home with a dead engine to land in a splintering of spars, twanging of wires and tearing of fabric, another little bit was rubbed away from what was left so that the callouses with which I'd covered myself began to wear very thin and there wasn't much left between the nerves and the daylight.

Someone started a party to celebrate the medals but at dinner the major came in with more orders for more of the same thing the next day and, instead, it fizzled out and we all went to bed early in the vain hope of getting some sleep. By this time, because we never knew where we were going to operate from next, our tenders and lorries roamed ahead of us, the drivers selecting fields and setting up the establishment in any old place among the neglected corn stooks, simply by shooing away the cattle and the people and burying the odd corpse that was lying about. We were moving now through countryside which had been occupied for four years by the Germans and the inscriptions on the houses showed how permanent they had thought their stay.

But there were other inscriptions, too – *Deutschland Kaput* – that stank of defeat and the same revulsion against the endless war that we were feeling. Black crêpe decorated German coats-of-arms and German soldiers were deserting now in dozens. Once I saw a team of German horses wearing German helmets led in by French women, but there were still plenty of bangs about, and from time to time a party of soldiers moving forward too confidently were wiped out by a vicious splattering of bullets from a clutch of desperate Germans determined not to go down without fighting; and occasionally, even though we lived well behind the line, we came across groups of dark hairy bodies where a machine gun burst had flattened a wagon team. The ground was unspoiled, however, though occasionally there was a huge scorched hole full of pulverized earth, or overgrown with vegetation blackening in the autumn rain. Occasionally even, there was an unburied German's boots among the undergrowth or sticking out from under a smashed pergola of roses left over from the summer.

It made the whole world seem devoid of humanity, somehow, and gave me a growing feeling of anxiety that began to worry me. I was desperately anxious to survive – though I was never sure what I was hoping to survive *for*, except to see Charley again – but I often felt that, with almost everyone I had known gone, I'd probably lived too long.

October faded in a flush of yellow sunlight that changed to mist. I got a letter from Sykes to say that the war in the Middle East was as good as over, and one from Charley to say she wished she were home and that I was home, too, and then, just when Jones and Munro and I were convincing ourselves that we were immune from the slaughter, Jones was hit while strafing a column of German troops hurrying eastwards. He seemed to fly straight into the fire of a machine gun and I saw flame come from under his machine. It was only small at first, but it grew larger and smoke began to trail behind him. He was almost low enough to put the machine down in a field and jump out but instead he seemed deliberately to crash into the column and the burning machine, flaring petrol and sparks and scraps of smouldering fabric and wood, tore into the column of men, wiping a dozen of them off the face of the earth before they could get out of its way, smashing them into bloody smears on the pavé as if they'd been a lot of flies on a window. When I got back, I jumped out of the machine to throw up, and I knew that I'd just about had enough. With the glimmer at the end of the long tunnel growing into the glare of daylight with the end of the misery, I didn't want to fly any more and I didn't want to kill any more. I felt I could have slept for days and couldn't believe sometimes that I was only weeks out of my teens and not yet officially an adult.

That night the major called me to his room. His face was hard. 'From tomorrow it's an all-out effort,' he said.

'Wasn't it today?' I said bitterly. 'And yesterday? And the day before that?'

He didn't look me in the face, and I knew he was hating it as much as I did. 'Every man who can get into the air must do so,' he said. 'They think we're going to end the war this year.'

'*This year?*' I couldn't believe my ears.

'That's what they say. They think there's a good chance the Germans'll throw their hand in. They're in trouble on the home front and they think that if they're not pushed hard enough they might recover, but that if we don't let up for a minute they'll decide they can't go on.'

'Oh, please God!' I breathed.

'Amen to that!' He picked up a sheet of paper and glanced at it. 'You're due for home establishment again,' he went on. 'So's Munro. So am I, for that matter. Curiously, though, I've got a feeling I'd like to be here when it all stops.'

'I think I would, too, sir.'

'Thought you might.' He sighed. 'What it means, though, is that we've got to chase the Germans everywhere they go, harry them whenever they try to stand, shoot their columns off the road and generally make life hell for them. The whole squadron's up from first light and I expect it'll be like that until they finally throw the towel in.'

—

We huddled by our aeroplanes next morning, waiting for it to grow light enough to take off by. I felt cold and wretched and decided that perhaps I was in for a dose of influenza, too, now, because the inside of the aeroplane suddenly seemed a soured stale place I no longer wished to see. I'd never managed to get to see Charley because, now, we'd moved on so much it was too far to go back to St

Marion, and it was impossible to telephone because of the demands being put on the hospitals by the wounded. I'd written her a hurried letter, though, telling her all about Marie-Ange and I'd even signed it for the first time 'with all my love,' which was quite a step forward, though I'd thought how small and inadequate a comment it seemed for such a big emotion.

I wasn't looking forward to what lay ahead. From what the major had told me it was going to be a desperate period of weariness but I had a feeling I could manage it for a bit longer if it was finally going to stop everything for good. Lloyd George had said we were fighting to make a land fit for heroes to live in but that hadn't cut much ice with me. Lloyd George was a politician and, after such a war as we'd been through, I felt I'd never trust another politician as long as I lived. Too many men had died to satisfy other men's political ambitions, and even while the Somme and Passchendaele had been going on all the politicians could do was squabble and manoeuvre to get the best they could for themselves and their stupid parties. Not very many of them had joined up either or even visited the front to see what it was like, so that Lloyd

George's slogans, clever as they were, didn't mean much to me.

After a while the major appeared and then I realized that the mechanics had wheeled out *his* machine, too. This time, it seemed 'every man' really meant 'every man'. I don't know what other commanding officers were doing, but ours was the sort to whom the words meant just what they said.

We were all carrying bombs and nobody pretended it was going to be easy because the German airfield at Merck was among the targets and we all knew German airfields had more machine guns on them these days than aeroplanes. A few of the men were making bantering remarks about narrow squeaks but nobody was laughing much, I noticed, and I buckled my belt carefully and adjusted my helmet and scarf with a conscious deliberation because I felt that if I didn't do it correctly, as I'd always done it, something might go wrong.

Munro appeared in front of me. He looked drawn and exhausted, his face taut and set like a drowning man clinging to some fragment of wreckage that preserved life. He'd been in France ever since 1915, first as an infantryman, and he'd served in the trenches and through the awful slaughter of the Somme. I wanted to say 'You've done enough' because I just didn't dare think of anything happening to him. He'd become a symbol for me and I felt that if anything did happen to him it could happen to me, too.

'Guid luck, Brat,' he said.

'Good luck, Jock.'

He frowned suddenly. 'Ah'm gettin' tae the stage when Ah feel Ah *need* a wee bitty luck,' he said. 'We've taken such a pastin' lately, mon, it's like some sort o' stinkin' rotten rope trick or somethin' – one moment a feller's there, the next he's gone.' He shrugged. 'All the same, if it ends soon and we can all settle down tae nine-tae-fivers and feet up on the hearth, I reckon I might just pull oot the stops a few more times.'

Everybody climbed into their machines and there was the crackle of Clerget engines starting up and the roar as the propellers started to rotate, dust blowing from behind the aeroplanes, blue smoke coughing from the exhaust stubs. A Very light curved up into the sky and chocks were jerked away so that the machines started to move into the middle of the field and roll forward over the uneven ground, tails up, wings rocking.

Over the line the sky was full of aeroplanes, despite the clouds, and we plastered Merck with everything we'd got. Aeroplanes and lorries were left burning and a hangar was flattened so that I knew there'd be no flying from there for a day or two, but the ground fire was hellish and I watched narrow-eyed as a Camel carried straight on down, hit the top of a parked lorry with its wheels, smashed into the ground and went sliding sideways, scattering bits of wreckage, until it hit a Fokker just pulling out in an attempt to get into the air, and the lot went up in a flare of flame from which I knew nobody would ever escape.

As we lifted into the sky, the Fokkers dropped on us like wolves on a flock of sheep while we bolted at low level for home. The SEs who were giving us top protection came down, too, and before I knew what was happening the whole crazy lot of us were wheeling and twisting towards the lines, only a few hundred feet above the ground so that every time I went round I could see faces everywhere, all turned upwards to watch.

We must have all been mad because eventually we drifted into the area of the highest point in the arc of shells on their way to and fro over the lines and, as the thought occurred to me, I found myself praying I wouldn't be hit by one of them as I'd once seen a BE hit in 1917 – just a flash and then a whole aeroplane and its crew splashed across the sky in falling fragments.

I saw a yellow Fokker fly into the ground at full speed, and rubbish and fragments of aeroplane hurtling into the air like the debris of an explosion, then an SE, far too low, went into a spin and was unable to pull out properly. It managed to level off but its wheels caught the wreckage of an old barn and it dropped into a shell hole and I saw the tail come up with a jerk.

Splinters flew from my centre section, and the Fokker I was firing at whirled away with smoke coming from under the cockpit, then I heard the usual crack-crack-crack of an enemy machine gun just behind me. In sheer terror I slithered sideways, just in time to see Munro's Camel limping painfully away towards the British lines with Munro hammering at a jammed gun. A Fokker pounced on him at once and I saw its guns going and the

Camel falter, then I smashed it away with pieces flying off the fuselage, just as I saw another from the corner of my eye coming round behind me and saw the smoke trails from his tracers going through the wings and heard the bullets hitting the engine cowling, and the clang as something went into the clockwork.

The engine note rose to a scream, then it began to grind as though everything inside was falling to pieces and getting chewed up, but for a moment I was safe and, glancing round for Munro, I saw his Camel just managing to float over what appeared to be the line, to hit the ground at a shallow angle. Skidding and sliding across the battered turf, it went first forwards, then sideways, then spun round to continue tail-first until it finally came to a rocking standstill, its wings and fuselage shredded, and as I levelled off I just had time to notice that Munro hadn't climbed out.

My engine was still groaning and clattering but I turned my head to chance another look. Just then, however, my controls went sloppy and I became too involved in saving my own skin to see what had happened to Munro. Glancing backwards, I saw one of my elevators was hanging off and fluttering behind on a wire and I could only guess that one of the whirling Fokkers had hit me without me realizing it as I passed, or that a splinter from one of the shells bursting close beneath had ripped it loose.

There wasn't much time to think about how it had happened, however, because I was fighting now to keep the machine from nose-diving. I was rapidly losing speed and as I nipped below a Fokker that came at me, I knew I wasn't going to be flying much longer. Someone drove the Fokker away and the sky suddenly cleared. A ruined house appeared in front of me and I was startled to realize I was so low, but I staggered past by a miracle, though the wing tip knocked off the chimney pot. Wires were trailing loose now and I saw the fabric across the whole lower plane begin to wrinkle as though the wing were moving, but I got the nose up again somehow and was just thinking I'd got away with it, when the engine cut dead and I hit the ground.

There was a hideous noise of breaking and splintering. I was flung forward against the safety belt and my head hit the windscreen as the machine bounced and lifted – flying still, but without its undercarriage – until she hit the ground again, while all I could do was hang on with both hands without a hope of controlling it. One blade of the propeller had broken off and the engine was screaming and shuddering as though trying to tear itself loose from the airframe. Wires were clattering all round me and pieces of wing and fuselage were dropping off in a shower, then I hit the ground again, lifted once more as though I couldn't stay down and, as my hands flickered over the knobs and switches, shutting off the engine and switching off the petrol and checking my safety belt, I hit the ground yet again, this time for good. The wings fell off and the engine dropped from its mountings then I hit the edge of a crater and the nose went down and the tail came up and over, and I found myself hanging upside-down in a blessed stillness.

The silence was bewildering as everything stopped moving and crashing and, with the blood rushing to my head, I could see that there seemed to be hardly anything left of the Camel beyond the piece I was sitting in. The wings had gone, the undercarriage and part of the tail had gone, and the engine had gone, too. How the remaining piece had stayed together to protect me I couldn't imagine. Then I became aware of the bursting of shells and the tapping of a machine gun and, without thinking, I released the safety belt and fell out on my head into soft mud. If it hadn't been soft I'd have broken my neck.

Two soldiers, their faces grimy with dirt, dragged me clear.

'You got shot down, mate?' one of them asked.

'You ain't bin out here long,' the other one said sarcastically. 'Y'oughta know they always land like that.'

I was in no mood to see the funny side of anything and, covered with shame at my fright, I cowered from the concussion of the shells. Then I remembered Munro and scrambled to my feet. Clambering to the edge of the shell-hole, I stared across the torn ground to where I could see his machine's tail sticking up through the smoke. There was a group of soldiers round it, their heads in the cockpit, and I ran towards it in my heavy flying boots, dodging and flinching at the bursting of shells and sweating under the leather coat.

Munro looked ghastly. His face was grey and there seemed to be blood everywhere, vivid against the pallor of his skin. His nose was bent round and there was a cut over one eye and a hole in his chin, so that as one of the soldiers poured water into his mouth it all came out again and ran down his neck to join the blood dripping on to his chest.

I was quite certain that he was already dead but his eyes opened and he saw me. He tried to say something but couldn't manage it and I felt helpless because I didn't know what he was trying to convey, then the soldiers lifted him out and laid him on the ground. Someone started shouting 'Stretcher bearers!' and in no time at all the stretcher was there. They seem to have got the rescue business better organized since they'd carried me off the field the previous year. Then, I'd had to scramble back mostly on my own, clutching my leg, half-dragged, half-pushed by Sykes and a couple of Highlanders through the shell holes until I could flop down in a sheltered ditch. Now, though, they had Munro moving back at full speed, with me alongside, sick with worry and knowing that the soldiers would consider I had the wind up. I had.

We fell into a shattered trench that seemed to be full of old unspeakable bodies, white as parchment, scrambled out at the other side, dived under a barbed wire entanglement, scuttled bent-double along the base of a broken wall and finally ended up in a sunken road where – blessed relief! – the shells didn't seem to be bursting. Behind a house, an ambulance was waiting, mud-spattered and grimy among a row of stretchers, its sides flecked by the marks of shell splinters. There was an infantry officer inside it who seemed to have stopped a machine-gun burst because there were small red patches all over his tunic and his breathing was swift and shallow.

A doctor examined Munro, then I saw him shake his head and a sergeant nodded at the stretcher bearers and they slid Munro into the ambulance. I was just about to climb in with him when the driver pushed me away. 'Sorry, sir,' he said. 'This is for the wounded.'

I stood back and dumbly watched the sergeant pull the canvas flaps down, then the engine started and it began to jolt off across the uneven road, so that I wondered what the poor devils inside must be feeling as their wounds were jolted.

I turned to the doctor. 'Will he be all right?' I asked.

'I don't know,' he said.

'Why not?'

'Because I didn't examine him.'

'Well, *why* didn't you examine him, you damn' fool?' I shrieked.

He stared at me for a moment then he put a hand on my shoulder. 'Because I don't have the time,' he said. 'That's why.' He indicated the stretchers lying all round him and it was only then that I realized how many there were. 'I've rather got my hands full. Was he a friend of yours?'

I felt like weeping. 'He's the only one I've got left,' I said numbly.

He patted my shoulder and turned away. A moment later he handed me a glass. 'Better drink this,' he said. 'You look as though you've had a bit of a fright yourself.'

The drink was neat brandy and it almost took the top off my head, but it bucked me up. I handed back the glass, said 'Thanks' and managed a smile.

'I decided the best thing I could do for him was get him away fast,' the doctor went on. 'Much better than keeping him here and trying to patch him up. It was touch and go and they've got more equipment back at base.'

'Yes,' I said. 'I understand now. Thanks. Sorry I made an ass of myself.'

He slapped my shoulder again and turned back to his work. An artillery officer from a nearby battery led me away and gave me a vast glass of whisky that made me choke after the brandy, then a big German cigar was stuck in my mouth and lit. I tried to say I didn't smoke but I was still gagging on the whisky, and the drink, the cigar, the shock and the fright were just too much.

'Excuse me,' I said and went out to be sick.

When I returned, wiping my mouth, my eyes streaming, the artillery officer looked sympathetically at me. 'Son,' he said, 'you look bloody awful.'

'I feel bloody awful,' I said. 'And it doesn't help when everybody keeps on calling me "son".'

He didn't seem to mind my rudeness and did all he could to help. Since there was nothing else to do but set off home, I trudged with the walking wounded through the mud and rubble and between the wreckage and the little clusters of bodies, until I reached brigade headquarters. Someone rang for a lorry and I was told to meet it at a village two miles further back. Someone offered me another drink but I shook my head and set off walking again. The lorry turned up eventually and I climbed in.

The driver said nothing, probably guessing how I was feeling, and we jolted back to the squadron.

The adjutant was the first person I saw. Everybody was in the mess when I arrived, and he was just leaving his office.

'Thank God you've turned up,' he said. 'You'd better get on the telephone.'

'Why?'

'The major didn't come back. They say he flew into some parked aeroplanes.'

'So that was the major,' I said. 'They got Munro as well, did you know?'

'Yes. We thought they'd got you, too. Somebody said they saw you hit a house. There's a new CO coming over in a couple of days but until then you're running the show again.'

I nodded and began to walk towards the office. This was the fourth time I'd had temporary command of a squadron so it didn't worry me because I knew what to do. I felt sorry about the major but with Munro it was different and I just couldn't face the thought. Munro and I had done two tours together – three, if you counted the one in Bloody April when they'd sent us all home early because the squadron had been decimated.

I just couldn't believe it. I felt numb and I didn't feel like eating so I didn't go near the mess and no one came near me. The other man in the hut, Jones' replacement, was still a stranger; I had nothing to say to him and fortunately he didn't try to start a conversation. Perhaps he guessed how I felt.

I felt a thousand years old and certain I'd never survive another day.

Chapter 10

As it happened, the weather was so awful the next day there was no flying at all, so I started ringing round the hospitals in the vicinity to find out if Munro had turned up. Nobody seemed to have heard of him and I could only imagine he'd died on the way back and they'd buried him somewhere alongside the road. In the end there was nothing for it but to break the news to Barbara Hatherley. I'd once promised I'd go personally but we were so far forward by this time it was impossible and even getting through to Charley by telephone took hours. I made it in the end, however, and she listened in silence while I told her, then I heard her make a little hiccoughing noise. 'Oh, Martin,' she said, 'how shall I do it?'

'I don't know,' I said wretchedly. 'But someone's got to and you'd be the best.'

It left me feeling as if the world had ended. It was just as Munro himself had once said – we were like gladiators, killing without feeling because it was our business, risking our lives for someone else's profit, doing it without emotion or pleasure or even excitement any longer. We'd been worn numb by fighting, and become stale with slaughter and soured by our trade.

Life had to go on, however, and in an effort to cheer us up, the next night the adjutant laid on a party in the mess on the flimsy excuse that the end of the war was near. It was the usual lunatic affair with crazy speeches and the behaviour of school-boys afterwards. Someone started a rugby match with the adjutant's hat and, with the squadron band playing *Orpheus In The Underworld* at top speed from the sidelines, more than a few bruises and black eyes were collected. Everybody felt better, however, because it let off a lot of steam and let loose a lot of the frustration everybody felt and, if the laughter was a little forced, as the drink flowed it gradually became more genuine and everybody stopped bothering to think. There was even someone who could play for a sing-song but, though he was red-hot on Chopin, he somehow hadn't the verve that

Munro had. I stayed to the end, determined like everyone else to dredge up every scrap of good cheer that was left, but I found when I reached my billet afterwards that I was stone-cold sober and curiously flattened in spirit.

It was November now and we knew the war couldn't last much longer. But peace just didn't seem possible after four long years, though it was being said now that the Germans had actually thrown in the towel at last and were asking for the fighting to stop, that the strikes in Germany were giving way even to mutiny in the fleet and that the soldiers were refusing to go to the front. I still found it hard to believe. There had been rumours of peace ever since the end of the Somme but nothing had ever come of them and, while it was obvious the Germans were beaten in France, I just didn't think they'd start screaming for mercy before they'd reached their own frontier.

The new major turned up the following morning. He walked with a stick and had three wound stripes and wasn't allowed to fly, and I began to wonder if, when the war was over, there'd be anything left but wreckage – wreckage of buildings, wreckage of machinery and wreckage of human beings. He asked me if I felt fit to go up because one of Munro's pilots had gone sick with flu and there was a spare machine. I didn't feel a bit like flying but I said I did and as I took off I could feel the bile of sickness in my throat, while my limbs seemed sluggish and heavy as though they didn't belong to me.

The cloud level was still solid and as we reached the front I saw unfinished German trenches, splintered trees, broken guns, burning stackyards where shells had fallen, and the bodies of horses and men. Shattered buildings with empty windows like sightless eyes lifted stark rafters up like the bones of a dead civilization as we roared over them, and every village seemed to be on fire and burning steadily under a pall of smoke. The pavé was shining with the rain, and the grey sky was reflected in the pools like fragments of silver.

Everywhere there seemed to be men in heavy coal-scuttle helmets trudging eastwards, their figures bent with weariness, and when they didn't even bother to look up, I couldn't bring myself to shoot at them. We dropped our bombs on a cluster of lorries by a railway siding and that was easier because the lorries seemed more impersonal than human beings. A few of the machines went round again to fire their guns and I saw vehicles burst into flames, but I couldn't do it myself and just sat above and waited for them to finish.

As we headed homewards, a few Fokkers came down on us but they seemed half-hearted. Two of them crashed into the ground all the same, and one of the Camels didn't make it back, but I saw the pilot climb out as it rolled itself into a ball of broken wood and fabric and thought 'Well, he won't have long to wait.' They probably wouldn't even bother to take him prisoner because, with the war going as it was, there was no longer any point.

When we landed, I sat in the cockpit, feeling the warmth from the engine and listening to the tick and creak of the cooling cylinders. I was so still the flight sergeant stuck his head over the side of the cockpit and asked if I were all right.

'Yes,' I said, 'I'm all right,' and I climbed out at last as if I were a cripple and dragged off my helmet to run a hand through my flattened hair.

I didn't think I could face another day but I was up twice the next morning. The night before I'd gone through my log book totting up just how many times I'd laid my head on the block, and the hours I'd flown in three years seemed astronomical. But so did the number of machines I'd smashed up crash-landing for one reason or other. However, since the number of German machines I'd destroyed seemed quite substantial, too, I decided that perhaps I'd probably earned my keep; though it was funny to think that if I'd become an architect on leaving school, as I'd intended, I wouldn't even have terminated my articles yet.

It seemed colder than it ought to have been, in spite of the November greyness, and I decided stupefaction was setting in. By evening, as we took off, the sky was heavy with lowbellied clouds. They were like wet sails, majestic and threatening, set above dark chasms and secret caves, but reaching up towards the light in ivory castles that were splendid in the last light of the day.

My eyes were roving restlessly about the reaches of the sky, because I was heavily conscious of the nearness of the end of the war and worried sick I'd miss those slow-shifting specks against the grey that meant Fokkers. Eventually we spotted a fight going on towards the east between a squadron of SEs and a host of Germans. The Fokkers seemed to have come out en masse for one last gamble before they were grounded for good and they were whirling like flies round a jampot. We smashed into the middle of them and from among the mêlée of coloured German wings and drab British ones, I saw aeroplanes falling limply away. My tiredness seemed to have left me, though, because going into a fight was always a little like plunging into an icy shower, the body cringing for the initiation but once in remarkably at ease.

A Fokker curved away in front of me, flames pouring from it, and I saw the pilot jump and go down in a whirl of arms and legs that made me feel sick as I thought how far he had to fall and what he must be thinking as he went down, then an SE literally staggered sideways in the sky as another Fokker caught it beam-on at point-blank range. Skidding about, I fired at an unexpected Triplane which had turned up from nowhere and swung round to find myself staring at the winking flashes of a Fokker's guns. For a fraction of a second I saw splinters fly all round me then I felt as though someone had hit me on top of the head with a hammer and everything went black.

When I came round I could feel warm blood running down my face and I couldn't see because it was filling my goggles. Through a red blur I saw the Camel was falling out of the sky and that if I didn't do something soon I'd be smashed to pieces like that poor devil I'd seen jump. Then I realized the Fokker that had hit me had followed me down and was still shooting at me and, even as I dragged the Camel's nose up, a bullet went through my forearm to jerk my hand from the stick and the Camel fell away again. Fortunately, someone spotted I was in trouble and the Fokker sheered off, and I fought through a blur of pain to get control. Changing hands, I pushed my goggles up and headed west. Every now and then I had to grip the joy stick with my knees to brush the blood from my eyes with my good hand and I could feel a warm coma of weariness flooding over me. I didn't feel in pain particularly, just aware of a numbing throb in my arm and a headache up top as if we'd had a party in the mess.

I decided quite calmly that I'd pushed my luck too far at last and that this time I was really going to die. The only thing I wanted was to do it among friends and I was terrified of becoming uncon-scious and losing control. But there were two other Camels with me now, one on either side of me, watching me every inch of the way to safety, and I thankfully saw the lines appear and slip behind me. The rubbish of the war passed beneath me and I could see fields now. I could have put the machine down in any of them but somehow I desperately wanted to reach the squadron. There was a doctor at hand there and this time I knew I wasn't going to be flying again the following morning and was going to need him.

I saw the field at last, an L-shaped piece of ground scored by wheels and tail-skids and lorry tyres. I didn't even attempt to circle it but went straight in. The wheels skimmed the trees and, fighting to keep my head up when it insisted on drooping to my chest, I put the machine down one-handed. But things were pretty blurred by this time and I misjudged it. I was going in left wing low and, as I tried to correct, I overdid it. The machine bounced, the right wing touched and then the Camel slewed round and went sliding sideways across the ground, crumpling the wings and shedding the undercarriage and tail in flying fragments. Gouging a great wound in the turf – which, oddly, I could see quite plainly, though I could hardly see even the cockpit in front of me – it finally slithered to a stop.

There was always the danger of fire after a crash and I didn't know whether I'd switched off the petrol. I could smell it everywhere and see smoke but I just didn't have the strength to do anything about it and simply sat there waiting for it to happen. Just then, though, I heard a car scream to a stop somewhere nearby and saw faces above me. Hands reached in and unfastened the belts, then they were dragging me none too tenderly from the cockpit before the whole thing went up in flames. They had me on my back and staring at the darkening evening sky when I heard a 'whuff' and saw the bright glare of fire, but I knew it was all right by this time and didn't even bother to think about it.

An ambulance appeared and I saw its light were on, then they lifted me on to a stretcher and I saw what was left of the daylight disappear as the stretcher was pushed into the ambulance. Someone gave me an injection and suddenly everything seemed all right. I didn't have to fly again and I could go to sleep at last.

—

When I came round I found myself staring at a nurse's face and I realized I was in hospital.

'Sykes! Sykes! He's awake!'

The voice seemed to come from a cavern just beyond the foot of the bed and I realized it was the nurse calling over her shoulder, then I saw Charley appear, her face drawn and anxious, and I decided that if she was around everything would be all right and simply faded away into sleep again.

When I came round again, my arm was strapped up and my head was bandaged and felt as though someone had been pounding it with a house brick. Charley was by the end of the bed, staring anxiously at the graph of my temperature, and as she saw me open my eyes she came nearer, a doubtful smile on her face.

'Am I going to live?' I asked.

'You'll be with us for a long time yet,' she said, and at last the doubt in her face gave way to a real grin. 'You only need a little tidying up on top.'

I felt very relieved. 'I think I want to go to sleep again,' I said. 'Do you mind?'

'Help yourself.' She came nearer and I decided she was going to kiss me, but then I passed out again so that I never had the pleasure of enjoying it.

When I finally emerged, there was no sign of Charley, only a ward full of nurses bustling up and down. This time I felt much more wide awake, but stiff as hell and with a head that felt as if it were ten other men's, all with hangovers. My mouth was dry and rasping and when someone came and gave me a drink of tea it tasted like heaven.

After a while I heard them calling for 'Sykes' again and eventually Charley appeared. 'Upsi-daisy,' she said pushing a pillow behind me. 'Well enough for some news?'

'Good or bad?' I asked.

'Good. Jock Munro turned up. There was some mix-up and he got lost. We found him at Bethune and Hatherley got him transferred here. He's in the next ward.'

I decided I must have died and gone to heaven after all, because this was too wonderful to be true. No more flying, not much pain, Charley at the end of the bed and Munro alive and only a few yards away.

'Good old Jock,' I murmured.

Charley smiled, her eyes bluer than I'd ever noticed. 'He's going to be all right,' she said. 'He was in a bit of a mess but they've stitched all the pieces together. Hatherley's satisfied, anyway. They've let her off work because all she can do is sit and look at him and weep with relief.'

'How about you sitting and weeping with relief over me?'

She laughed. 'Not likely. You'll always survive. It's worth a guinea a box just to see you coming up again, dudgeon in every step, ready for the next round.'

'Not this time,' I murmured. 'This time I thought I was dead and buried, with the worms doing eyes-right and fours-about between my ribs.'

She bent and stared at me. 'They say it's almost over, Martin,' she went on. 'They say it's going to stop any time now. The Canadians are heading for Mons. It'll be funny if they reach it, won't it, just when the Hun throws in the towel? Right back where it all started. Just to show what an unholy waste of money, effort and lives the last four years have been.'

Someone called her away then, but I didn't mind. It was enough just to have her near. I was glad that Munro had made it. He deserved to survive, though I was sorry that Marie-Ange was going to have to get herself married without me as best man, after all. Judging by the look of things, they'd be sending me home as soon as I was fit to travel.

The following morning they took me into the operating theatre and took out a few bits of bone that were floating around loose under my scalp, and when I came out of the anaesthetic my head hurt like hell and I was low in spirits. For no reason at all I began to think of myself as I'd been when the war had started, just a boy with no greater ambition than to score a few runs in a school cricket match, and then of myself as I was at that moment, miserable, worn out, very nearly devoid of strength, ambition or even the will to live, yet officially still not an adult. By the time the anaesthetic had worn off completely, I was feeling thoroughly wretched and wishing Charley would appear.

Just as she did so, I heard bangs going off outside, and a nurse ran into the ward. 'Sykes! Sykes! Can you hear the maroons? It's over — it's really all over! Are you coming out to see what's happening?'

Charley shook her head. 'No, I'll stay here, I think,' she said, but the noises outside increased and I could hear shouting and a lot of laughter, and someone playing on a trumpet that seemed to be all out of tune. It was all over at last. It really was.

All the way from Switzerland to the sea it had all come to a stop. All the way from Albert to St Quentin, from Arras to Cambrai and Le Cateau, the land was suddenly still and in the misty autumn day I felt that after the din the silence must be thunderous, like being buried alive. Because, amid all the wreckage of the war, the crosses still lay in the fields and gardens and woods all the way through the fighting zone, as though every misery of the last four years were rising to remind us all of what had happened, as though people we'd known and lost were calling out to us not to forget them.

I thought of my brother and Frank Griffiths and Wickitt, who were all I could remember of my first tour, and then of Catlow and Bull and Major Latta of the second, and Ludo Sykes and Munro who'd overlapped into a third and a fourth with Taffy Jones and Milne and a few others, and then it dawned on me properly that there was to be no more of it. It was ended. It really was, and I could go home and start getting back to what I was going to do with my life – whatever it was.

I felt so relieved for a moment I couldn't get my breath, and I drew two or three great gulping gasps of air that turned into sobs, and suddenly I realized I was crying. Not loudly. Not even at all really. Just lying there, wet-eyed, feeling desperately sorry for myself and stupidly unable to stop the prickling behind my eyes. Charley saw me and hurried across so that I had to turn my head, trying not to let her see. But she'd always had sharp eyes and there wasn't much she missed.

She put her hand on mine and stared into my face. 'Why?' she asked. 'Why, Martin? It's all over.'

That was why, of course. Because it *was* all over. And because I was tired. And because of Taffy Jones and Bull and the people who hadn't come through. And because I had.

I managed a smile. 'It's nothing,' I said. 'Just a spot of boozer's gloom or something. I'll be all right in a minute.'

She bent closer. 'Just think, Martin,' she said. 'We'll all be going home.'

'We'll tell some whoppers then, Charley. How we won the war. Me with all my brass and you with your putty medal.'

I could see her eyes sparkling as though they were damp. 'Twenty years from now,' she said, 'everybody'll be so bored with us they'll dodge when they see us coming.'

'Can't say I'll mind,' I murmured. 'So long as I'm still around. I never thought I would be.'